Infa

Monkton Abbeyfields

Infamous Rival

Coronet Press

~

Copyright © Francine Howarth 2019

One

Georgette drew her velvet cloak tight about her whilst glancing out at the forbidding moonlit landscape. She was rather glad the horses were keeping to a steady trot, for her previous sense of excitement was now overshadowed by anguish and dread.

She knew the private drag was passing close to Monkton Abbeyfields. The locale all too familiar, and yet, it was so silly to be feeling anxious. Adam Brockenbury simply could not be in residence at Abbeyfields. After all, he was spied at White's Chocolate House only yesterday, and her grandfather had overheard news of Adam's engagement at a dinner party that very evening. It was also common knowledge Adam was due at Blenheim Palace for a grand masque ball of Friday next.

Nevertheless, of all the men in London, Adam Brockenbury remained the one man she wished never to set eyes on ever again. Such avoidance was easily accomplished within the great metropolis. In the City of Bath everyone knew everyone else, and it was less easy to travel about incognito. Should Adam for any reason return to Batheaston on the Saturday, she would be long gone from Fenemore Cottage by then, for Abbeyfields itself remained a disquieting reminder of her last trip to this part of the Avon Valley.

She cast a fleeting glance at her travelling companion; a perfect gentleman in every way, thus conversation en route had proved most convivial. Nonetheless, silence had descended for the last mile or so.

It was inappropriate to watch a sleeping man but rather pleasing; his head slightly forward, chin resting on lace-trimmed cravat, his shoulder wedged against the window. He seemed none the worse for the odd jolt or two as the coach swayed and rattled over ruts, and in all their conversations she had not established his name, nor thought to ask.

He was as she had seen a man of broad shoulders yet slim of form and of goodly height; the latter belied when seated. His handsome face, although a mite grave whilst in argument with the booking agent had immediately creased with smiles most charming upon her suggestion they might care to share the drag. All despite both had assumed private hire of said coach, and neither a shared arrangement in mind.

In retrospect, it was all rather strange how a mistake could have occurred with the booking in the first place, for the coaching company had long since gained excellent reputation for discretion and efficiency. Nonetheless a mistake had occurred, and as they were travelling to almost the same destination it had seemed only polite to offer him a seat even though he had offered to give sway to her and wait another day. Such grace had seemed contradictory when in heated exchange at the coaching inn, his grey eyes had implied murderous thoughts toward the booking clerk, though manner alluding otherwise.

She glanced again through the window; frost glittering on hedgerows and grass of outlying fields. Jack Frost had also begun crafting beautiful pictures on the coach glass as though embalming them in his icy grip. Barely able to feel her toes despite a fleece-lined rug about her knees, she moved each foot in turn and rubbed gloved hands together; all the while her breath lingered on the ether.

How foolhardy to have undertaken the journey at all, but it was too late now to turn back and seek a warm hearth at a wayside inn. Fenemore lay no more than a mile hence, and at least her arrival so late in the evening would likely pass unnoticed by villagers.

Once she was safe within the confines of Fenemore, who could possibly know she was there? As far as she was aware her travelling companion was bound for Bath not Batheaston, so encounter with each other again was quite unlikely for she had no intention of parading herself in public places. And when she again departed under cover of darkness come Friday, her stay would bring no shame to bear on the Knightleys.

With her reputation sufficiently ruined in the County of Somerset, invitations to houses of note would never come her way. And yet, for several seasons prior to her disgrace her presence had been sought quite regular by wealthy parents eager to see their sons wed to a lady of high rank and substantial dowry.

She had her dowry as before. *But who would wed her now?*

How thankful she was her grandfather had never believed a word put about by Adam Brockenbury, at her having had a hand in his elder brother's untimely death. It was all so unfair. She had barely known James Brockenbury other than a mere acquaintance of her lady friends, and no prior inkling he was going to declare undying love and ask for her hand in marriage. Such was his drunken enthusiasm he dragged her into the garden at Abbeyfields, and thence to the stable yard for a so-called elopement. Utter madness.

With no recourse but to say she did not wish to marry him she had asked him to go away. *What else was there to say to a man so inebriated he could barely stand upright?* With his brother in attendance and several other young men gathered around it was plain to see he was in no fit state and better they had put him to bed. But no, they had set about to tease and taunt him and it all became quite frightening to be penned in by them, and all whilst his younger brother aided and abetted in their silly game.

She had not flirted with James on that fateful night. Nor had she with Adam, whom she had not liked once his rakish manners were made known to her. And to suggest she had dared to have a hand in their drunkenness was utter nonsense. Blame of that kind fell solidly on the shoulders of Adam, who became heir apparent to the Brockenbury fortune on that very black night. If not for the shock of it all she would have accused Adam of murder, for he was the last person to see James alive.

She shivered. The memory of James' fate was too awful to dwell upon, and her own equally unbearable. Oh yes, Adam Brockenbury was the very devil incarnate, and his father would forever remain unaware of the truth. Adam, despicable Adam, had brutally induced a pact of silence and allegiance between him and the other young men of his attendance.

How dreadful it all was, as poor James lay dying in the arms of one of Adam's friends. And worse, she then dragged to the stable loft in pretence at hiding her, supposedly to save her from the outright shame of being caught in the company of so many men. But it was all a ploy and Adam then leapt astride her with intent. If not for the head groom roused from his bed due to the ribaldry of Adam's friends and that of a pistol fired, her fate might have been far worse than that of escape from the loft with just her hair in disarray.

Nothing said in her own defence had lessened outrageous accusations she was little more than a trollop. Her host, Lord Brockenbury, had ordered her to leave with immediate effect, the shame of her episode in the hayloft then recounted and exaggerated upon throughout the county, her reputation thus in tatters.

She had every reason to loathe Adam Brockenbury for he had ruined her life. Her only friends were that of the Knightley girls, who had refused to believe his account of her having jilted James and thrown herself at Adam. Neither had believed James had any reason to take his own life. It was all so terrible, so shocking and so unexpected.

Aware the horses had begun to slow their pace she surmised they were on approach to the bridge, the Avon before them. She braced herself, for it always felt as though her stomach collided with heart when crossing humpback bridges.

As the horses once again settled to a steady trot, the coach suddenly lurched as though its wheels had passed over something in its path. Thrust sideways her companion's head banged against the window; she likewise thus thrown to her left and now stretched out across the seat opposite to his.

"Damnation," declared he, clutching at his head. "What happened?"

"I think we shall know soon enough, for the coach is slowing down."

She pushed herself upright, terrible thoughts milling in her head. *Was someone lying hurt and injured?*

The coach finally came to a standstill and within seconds her companion had the door open and shouted up to the coachman. "Why have we stopped?"

The coachman's reply, "We rode o'er somethin' on the highway back a ways."

"Did you not see what it was?"

"Nah, not a thing for 'twas too dark, sir. But Jim is a going to see what it were."

"Good God, man. A moonlit night. Frost on the ground and almost as bright as day. How could you not see whatever in your path?"

"I tells yer I didn't see nothin' so it must have come at us from them there trees back away, by the bridge, 'cause twer rear wheel as run o'er it. What 'ere it be."

Her companion alighted from the coach and walked back along the highway. Although curious she decided it was best to stay wrapped up and await news of what had caused the coach to lurch so badly. It seemed an age before he returned, along with the armed guard who immediately clambered up beside the coachman. In silence her companion stepped aboard, and upon closing the door and retaking his seat he shook his head in the manner of no hope afforded the victim of the collision.

"I can only guess it was not a person, for surely we would not drive on with somebody left lying dead or wounded on the highway."

"We lay it on the verge, and I shall arrange for it to be picked up first thing in the morning." The coach lurched and then proceeded onward. "Little harm will befall the poor creature on a night such this."

"May I ask what it is?"

"A hound. Why it was out and about is strange indeed. I cannot recall its ever deserting my father's side."

Her stomach tightened. Breath caught in her throat, as dread and fear gripped her. *Oh no, not a son of Abbeyfields.* "You live near here?"

"Indeed I do," his reply, his grey eyes levelled on hers. "I fear I have been somewhat lax with introduction, despite our having conversed in genial spirit. May I say, the tinkling ring of your voice is most delightful and sweet music to the ears, unlike the caustic tones of erstwhile colleagues and that of my clerk."

If not in fear of who he might be, she could well have laughed in coquettish manner at his bold inference, for he'd fallen asleep whilst she left animated in discourse. Instead her tongue rallied quite sharp, "And you are?"

"Edwin Brockenbury."

Her heart raced, bile rising in throat and silence became deafening. She could not muster a word, her thoughts colliding with memories, yet try as she might she could not recall Edwin Brockenbury's face as one of those present on the night of James Brockenbury's tragic death.

"Does the name Brockenbury distress you?" He leaned forward elbow to knee, hesitant in manner, his face rigid calm; though genuine concern etched thereon. "Reaction such as yours is not that uncommon. My brother it seems is wont to leave a trail of broken hearts countrywide, which *has* rather tarnished the name Brockenbury. Hence, Ranulph and I are forced to suffer the consequences of bitter tongued beauties when introduced at social functions."

"Broken heart—Me, with broken heart and left in Adam's wake? I think not."

"Forgive me, please. I had no right to suggest or imply you might harbour bad feeling toward a Brockenbury."

He sat back, his eyes not leaving hers for a second and it was most disconcerting; but in a nice way. Throughout the journey air of authority and reserved calm had emanated from his very person, though his caring manner at the coaching inn had won her respect or they would not now be sharing the drag. His deep timbre of voice, too, had sounded sincere, and not once had it raised sense of alarm to falseness nor implied him a man of ill repute during brief rests at wayside inns along the way.

She had to say something. Break the silence. For he looked most concerned that he had wrong-footed her and made bold on wild assumption.

"No, please, forgive me. Supposition is unwise at the best of times, and our journey, until the accident, indeed, was most pleasant. To have company on a long journey always lessens what is otherwise a tedious and lonely experience."

A tentative smile creased his face. "In that case, would you mind terribly if I leap from the coach at the gates to Abbeyfields?"

"At the gates? Not to be driven to the house in style?" In response he chuckled, a deep-throated chuckle. In other circumstances such might have caused her heart to flutter. "Please, you cannot walk in these freezing conditions."

"I fear you are chilled enough young lady, so home with you straight away. I'll not freeze to death trudging the drive to the house. As it is, the hound's death has raised a needling question as to why he was where he was at the time of his death," said he, reaching for his gold-topped cane previously abandoned on the seat beside him.

She had already surmised it to be a swordstick, its dragon's head handle ornate and curved to fit neat to palm of hand; which he promptly used to thump the roof of the drag, his expression erring curiosity. "Shall you be at Fenemore for a long or short stay?"

Her heart lurched. "How did you know I am to stay at Fenemore?"

"You booked for a drive from London to Fenemore Batheaston, and I too from London to a nearby destination. When I arrived at the inn it was assumed *I* was the passenger for Fenemore. Hence your arrival coincided with and interrupted a heated argument, that I too, happened to be bound for Batheaston, but it was Abbeyfields itself I wished to be taken to." A smile creased his face. "I am not sure how, but you seemed to think my intended journey was

8

to Bath. And gentleman that I am I chose not to reveal otherwise."

"So you had intended escorting me to Fenemore and then returning to Abbeyfields?" She laughed. "Oh how gallant, and now you wish to leap from the coach and abandon me."

She immediately corrected her outburst. "*Please*, I do beg your forgiveness. That sounded terribly remiss, when you must be quite worried about your father."

Aware the drag was slowing down with verbal encouragement to the horses from the coachman, Edwin Brockenbury once again leaned forward; and this time he extended his hand. She accepted his gesture of friendship their kid gloves coming together, and not for one minute had she expected him to dip his head and kiss her gloved fingers.

The contact was fleeting, but when his eyes levelled on hers something indefinable sparkled within and, "Good night, Lady Beaumont," came as quite a shock. Nonetheless his smile was enough to melt the coldest of lady's heart, and as reassuring as were his final words: "Be assured your presence at Fenemore will not slip from my tongue."

With that he departed and closed the door and disappeared from view. So he had known her identity all along and said not a word. He was most certainly nothing like his hateful brother. She could, if he were not a Brockenbury be quite taken with him.

It was all but a few moments before the drag moved off and there he was standing in front of magnificent wrought iron gates, a large leather valise at his feet. He waved, turned, pushed one of the gates and that was her last sighting of him.

Yes indeed. There was something about Edwin Brockenbury that was most appealing. But, who was he really? For all she knew he could be a married man. After all, who would say no to a man of his looks, good manners, and those haunting grey eyes?

Two

Damn. It was perishing cold.

Feeling a mite ill-mannered in not having revealed his name until called upon to do so had ensured a peaceful journey with a thoroughly pleasant and highly attractive lady. Her secret was indeed safe with him. He had no desire to disclose her presence at Fenemore.

He closed the gate and strode at a brisk pace along the drive. A speck of light in the distance was the only beacon that Abbeyfields lay ahead. Every footstep announced his presence to wildlife and that of sheep grazing a nearby paddock. A bleat here and there echoed through the stillness of the land; a barn owl screeched; a dog fox barked and once again the only sound was that of iced ground crunching beneath his boots: his every tread bringing a distant beacon of light closer.

At a guess he could well understand why the lady had chosen to arrive cloaked in darkness, when her journey could have been broken with overnight stay at any number of coaching inns en route. Such was commonplace with ladies when travelling, more especially those whom he had dallied with, who were prone to need rest overnight and to freshen up on long journeys besides partaking of sustenance. But Lady Beaumont's presence back in Somerset would soon set tongues wagging, if her whereabouts were to become general knowledge.

He drew a deep breath, the chill air invigorating, but not as sweetly stimulating as the essence of lavender within the coach, which had proved almost as heady as the joy of watching his travelling companion's delightfully kissable lips play with words. Her green eyes too, as enchanting as a

11

woodland glade basking in sunlight, and the sheer thought of coiling her fair ringlets around his fingers had passed the time in pleasurable pursuits whilst asleep.

If he was now reading the situation correct, the lady had wished to enter and leave Fenemore without Adam hearing of her presence so close to Abbeyfields. Without doubt, Georgette— Lady Georgette Beaumont was a shrewd young woman, but a little too honest for her own good. It would have been wise to have travelled under a nom de plume. Instead she had booked the drag for a Miss Beaumont as opposed to titled grandee, as was her rank. Tongues might yet wag when the coachman and guard took shelter for themselves and the horses at the local coaching inn. After all, farm hands at Abbeyfields were familiar with the local innkeeper; and a regular glass of ale or cider quaffed in passing was seen as fair exchange for a brace of rabbits.

He smiled for although his father was a hard taskmaster never had he begrudged his farm labourers bartering with rabbit meat in exchange for whatever needs arose within their individual households. His father despised rabbits with a vengeance and had wasted many hours popping off at them with pistols, though he favoured a blunderbuss that was apt to knock him over when too much port was the driving force.

Sufficiently close to the house he could see the beacon of light was casting from the front entrance rather than from un-shuttered windows. People with lanterns were scurrying from the stable yard and assembling out front of the house. It was only natural to suppose something was wrong, for why else would men with lanterns be gathering en masse? He rushed forward at the run, and immediately sensed air of relief emanating from the assembled as soon as they spied him on approach.

"Oh, young Master Edwin. I be so glad to see you," said the farm bailiff. "Your father be out there somewhere and no one do rightly know where. He failed to come back for dinner, and we already be'n up the hill and through the copse, and we's about to go to the river path."

He let fall his valise from grasp for Caesar's untimely death had already given rise to element of concern, but not of this kind. "Here, give me a lantern. I think I might know in which direction he went."

A farmhand passed over a lantern and he quickly led off, his father's men at his back. Vaulting over the park railings, the men scrambling after him; he shouted back, "Caesar collided with the coach I was travelling on tonight. Poor animal went under the wheel and is lying dead on the verge."

A young farmhand caught him up and kept astride of him. "That's a shame sir, 'cause Caesar was a good and faithful friend to his lordship."

It was that precise aspect of the hound's faithfulness that worried him, for in normal circumstances his father and Caesar were never apart. The hound went everywhere with him: to town, to his club, even to houses of friends. He could not believe it likely the hound had sought help from him; that Caesar had scented him within the coach. Surely that was impossible?

He could see the tree line ahead where Caesar had scrambled through the hedge and lumbered into the coach. Upon a thorough search of that stretch of the hedge there was no sign of his father. He called out, and every man with him stood still in hope of some sort of response but there was no sound bar the breathing of many men. "Split up, men, spread out and we shall all walk toward the east, and if we find nothing we go west."

The men quickly spread out across the field in a line and set off at a steady walk, and it was not long before the alarm was raised near to the hedge adjoining the river. They had found him, but not as expected. He might have been drunk when he had set out with a gun in hand but his death was no accident. He had a dagger embedded in his chest.

"Master Edwin, this is bad," said the bailiff. "Who could have done such a thing and why for?"

"I cannot think of anyone who hated father sufficient in wont to kill him. Yes, there were those that might have harboured minor grievances, but of the few, not any one of them would resort to murder. I have no idea who did this, Joseph, no idea at all."

"He were 'appy enough this afternoon when Master Adam were 'ere."

"Adam was here, but I— I thought him in London until Friday."

"Oooh no, sir. He went into Bath just afore nightfall. I passed him on me way home and he said as how yer father were wont to stay out shootin' so he might as well go and dine with friends."

Tears suddenly welled and the men's faces became a blur, but his thoughts were as much about Caesar as that of his father. He wiped his eyes, and Joseph said in a soft and kindly voice, "Go on back, Sir. We'll bring his lordship home."

"No, I'll help, for even though he didn't much approve of my chosen path in life, he's my father and we had a happy enough relationship despite our differences."

"Ah well, I'd say he were right proud of you. I heard 'n tell many a visitor you's a lawyer in posh chambers and do demand, or were it do command high revenue?"

He almost laughed. "Aye Joseph, 'tis a rich man or woman who can afford my services. Though I'm not averse to helping a poor soul, when I think of them as deserving of help."

"Let's be getting him home, then Sir."

Three

They were her treasured friends.

With red-hot coals in the hearth Beatrice set to with toasting muffins; her ringlets glowing bright as shiny copper; her pale skin flushed pink; her gown of dark blue matching her eyes. How strange it all seemed, for the Knightley girls loved to toast bread or muffins themselves, the parlour maid dismissed. It was a special time, a private time for catching up on gossip from around the county.

In all fairness Rose and Beatrice had not pressed for tittle-tattle the previous evening and throughout the day had held their tongues in check. Nevertheless, she sensed they were bursting for news of London society, and it came as little surprise when Rose spoke her thoughts: "Georgette, are you happy residing in London?"

"It serves its purpose, though I rarely venture beyond the grounds of the house whilst ladies of the *ton* are at play. I have no exciting news to impart of dinner parties, balls or civic functions, nor that of theatres and the like. Of course I do have visitors and I do engage with high-borne elderly ladies of the *haut ton*. The Duchess of Norfleet, for one, who refers to *ton* antics as akin to the theatre and dreadful dramatics of pushy upstart mothers, all of whom foist unsuitable gals onto equally unsuitable beaux."

Rose cast a cheery smile. "Can you not come out of hiding? What happened on that dreadful night at Abbeyfields; if not entirely forgotten, it is barely mentioned hereabouts. I feel sure every lady present on that tragic evening must have sighed with relief it was not they whom Adam cornered. And goodness,

London must be awash with scandals of one sort or

another."

"I do get out and about in grandfather's barouche early of morn, when the ladies of the *ton* are still ensconced in their boudoirs. Though I do take walks in Hyde Park of an evening, when of course those same ladies are busy in preparation for dinner engagements and the like, except those out for secret liaisons with lovers. Fortunately, such are equal in seeking anonymity."

Rose' violet eyes flashed wide. "Oh do tell. Who have you seen and with whom were they gallivanting?"

She laughed at this from Rose and the childlike way in which her dearest friend leaned forward as though expecting whispered revelations. "You are both gluttons for gossip."

Beatrice burst into laughter; the first half of a muffin toasted and hastily plopped on a plate, her eyes levelled on Rose. "What else do you expect from a woman in her ungainly state, and unwilling to poke her nose beyond the garden gate?"

"I am neither ungainly of leg, nor ungamely, which is a sporting term young bucks use when referring to young women of fulsome proportions." challenged Rose. "I am considerably with child and do not wish to be seen this way. As soon as I have—" She placed her hand to swollen bump. "When it is born I shall again walk out."

Beatrice returned to the toasting of halved muffins. "Eat up dear sister, for yon soldier baby needs nourishment."

"Soldier baby?"

"What else can it be?" said Beatrice, a smirk. "You said yourself '*it marches on a full belly*'."

Rose' face creased into a smile, a dreamy faraway look to eye and finger twirling a loose auburn curl. "If it is a soldier boy, Frederick will be thrilled to receive such glad tidings."

Beatrice giggled. "Just imagine how well the baby's head will be wetted?"

Rose sat up straight, her smile gone. "Frederick is no drunkard."

"I did not say he was," batted her sister, "but soldiers will be soldiers, and officers are no better than their men when their manliness is proven with a son and heir the first born."

The banter between the sisters was most entertaining and afforded Georgette respite from Rose' interest in London and her life there: such as it was. It was true she had not wished to meet with outright scorn and whispers. Avoidance of gentlemen out for early morning canters and those taking evening strolls for the most part had proved successful, but she had inevitably met the odd one or two familiar faces. They had not, as expected, shunned her and instead had doffed their hats and smiled openly and not a sneer from any one of them.

Perhaps it was indeed time to come out of hiding, and perhaps a trip out, all together, would be beneficial for Rose, too. Although a little over seven months with child she looked no more than a little fulsome in bosom and not nearly as roundly pronounced in middling matters as she imagined.

"What about a trip to Wells? We could stay at the White Hart. It has lovely fare and comfortable rooms. And we could attend service at the Cathedral. The choristers there are second to none."

"The White Hart?" Rose looked aghast at such a suggestion. "We have relations at Dulcote and Dinder."

"And we are most welcome to stay at either household when we so choose," chirped Beatrice; whilst Rose hurriedly buttered a toasted half muffin. "I can write a letter to each aunt, and then we can plan what we shall do and what we shall see."

"Oh the walk from Dulcote to Wells across park fields will be such fun," said Rose. "No carriages to dodge. No horsemen, either. "Have you walked them, Georgette?"

"No, but I did take a guided walk up to red rocks and through the woods. Though confess the walk around the palace moat was by far of more interest, so too a stroll through the cathedral cloisters."

"That is what we shall do, then. We shall retrace all our steps. Each and every one," declared Rose. "Just as soon as we know for sure we can stay with either the Walkers or the Melrose family."

Beatrice wiped her brow with the back of her hand. "Phew, I am almost as toasted as the muffins."

Loud knocking on the front door startled them, and the two Knightley's looked one to the other, then Rose said, "Oh my goodness. We forgot about Ranulph. It's your first sitting today."

Beatrice looked horrified. "Oh no, I cannot, cannot be painted when I am all hot and red in the face." She fanned her face with hands, scrambled to her feet and fled the room, her last words: "Feed him muffins and tell him I will be down shortly."

"I am so sorry Georgette," said Rose, "but it seems we are to entertain Ranulph Brockenbury whilst Beatrice freshens up a little."

"A Brockenbury?"

Rose leaned close and whispered, "A Brockenbury, yes, but I promise, you will like him. He is so sweet and has quite a serious awkwardness."

With bated breath they awaited Ranulph's entrance, and it was no more than minutes before Mr. Knightley's manservant announced the young gentleman, and duly closed the door behind him.

She could see Ranulph's disfigurement for herself, and was rather glad Rose had forewarned her. He walked with an unusual gait, the twist of his spine therefore notable. His face on the other hand was rather fetching and not unlike Edwin Brockenbury's, though less grave. Of slight build, of middling height due to his spinal malfunction, his eyes were dark blue and a wicked twinkle therein. While his red-gold curls were wholly at odds to the rest of his clan: all dark and dour.

His polite bow appeared difficult to accomplish, and implied it a painful exercise, as he said, "Mrs. Davenport, and as beautiful as ever."

Rose blushed. "Shame on you Ranulph, for such wicked flattery of a married woman."

"Two beautiful women," he said, flashing a big smile. "I fear I intrude."

"Not at all, dearest fellow, and this is my dear friend, Lady Georgette Beaumont."

Ranulph's eyes widened, his mouth fell open and not a word came forth. It was fair to assume he felt a mite awkward, her name renowned.

He nonetheless rallied and hand outstretched strode forward. "Your ladyship, my pleasure." He bowed again, and his smile returned upon brief touching of their hands. "Please believe me when I say I bear no ill will whatsoever toward you. I confess to no understanding of what occurred between yourself and my late brother, but on seeing your beauty I shall think of you as a victim of injustice and of Adam's scorn."

She forced a smile, unease gripping her despite his kindness. "I thank you for your brave honesty, and although I stand the accused, I remain as much at a loss as everyone else as to what occurred on that fateful evening. I swear I barely knew James."

"I can vouch for that, Ranulph. It was Georgette's first introduction to James."

"Then I shall believe you are absolute in innocence of all the charges laid against you." He smiled; a captivatingly charming smile. "I confess I am no lawyer nor judge, for one in the family is sufficient methinks."

Edwin Brockenbury's judicious directive of events prior to their journey from London leapt to the forefront of her mind. "By that, do you mean your brother Edwin is a man of law?"

"That he is my lady. Kings Council and Judge-in-waiting, though his wait is likely no more than a few weeks hence." He chuckled. "Again, I shall say, two beautiful women."

"Do not even think it," said Rose, as he glanced across at her, "I will not be put to canvas until the baby is safe in its cradle. Now, come and butter this muffin and eat it all up, there's a good boy."

"Yes mother," his mischievous reply, as he slid awkward to the chair beside the afternoon tea table.

Rose laughed, stabbed another half muffin with her toasting fork and thrust it to the glowing hearth. "You do know Beatrice will boss you mercilessly when you are married."

"Married?"

"Yes, married. You are going to propose, are you not?"

He looked somewhat askance but nevertheless buttered his muffin, and then in downhearted tone, said, "Well— No. I had not thought she would think me fitting."

"Fitting? What is fitting? You are young and—" Rose looked at him then, her cheeks flushed from the fire. "Able, are you not, to make her happy in every way?"

He almost choked on his first bite taken of the muffin, and then laughed. "If I am to understand by able, you mean to father a child, then yes, I am able."

"Good," said Rose, her attention back to almost scorched muffin, which she hastily turned on the fork and again placed to the fire. "That's settled then, and I shall leave it to you to decide when you shall ask her."

"Thank you, I appreciate your forbearance in granting me right to ask for your sister's hand, but I fear I must first seek approval from Mr. Knightley."

"Father will agree. No fear of that, Ranulph." Rose glanced up, a smile on her face. "Don't you think they will make for a grand couple, Georgette?"

It was bad enough having to listen to intimate and bizarre conversation betwixt the pair: *now she was expected to pass comment?*

"I suspect Mr. Brockenbury and Beatrice know their own minds and a happy conclusion will result, if they so wish it."

"They wish it, but neither will say it." The muffin was now scorched on both sides. "Oh dear, it's over done."

Ranulph rallied to her aid. "As the only man in the room I shall be gallant and partake of the burnt muffin."

Rose immediately popped it onto Ranulph's plate. "Sweet boy, and if I were not wed and not with child, I would gladly be your wife."

He laughed. "Alas, my heart belongs to Beatrice."

At that very moment the young lady waltzed into the room; his words still hanging in the air. As their eyes met what passed between them could not be mistaken as anything but love for each other.

"There Georgette," declared Rose, appraising the pair. "Do you not agree they are made for each other?"

Rose, once so reserved and cordial of manner, had now become forthright in every word spoken. *Was this what marriage to a soldier did to a young woman*? Not that a reply was of necessity for Beatrice stole the moment.

"You promised, Rose, promised you would not breathe a word of my affections for Ranulph." Beatrice fair glared at her sister, her cheeks flaming along with Ranulph's. The pair clearly felt compromised and seeming unsure who should take the lead. He did open his mouth as though to speak just at the point Beatrice burst into tears and blubbered, "You did this on purpose, and now Ranulph will think me a silly little mouse. One who cannot speak for herself, and I *hate* you, *hate* you."

Beatrice turned and fled, and Rose' face turned ashen.

"B, *wait*. Please, *please* don't rush off. My intention was not to offend. I love you, love both of you, and all I wanted—"

Rose's words fell on empty space, the door left ajar and Beatrice gone.

Ranulph eased himself from the chair and all but straightened his spine. "May I go to her?"

Rose nodded in acquiescence. "I am so sorry Ranulph. I had thought to hasten a romance in the making and a happy outcome would be the result this very afternoon."

"Perhaps I can save the day," said he, in courteous response mid bow.

As he left the room tears brimmed and Rose looked utterly crestfallen. "Oh Georgette, what a foolish, foolish thing I have done. She was so upset."

"A little foolhardy, perhaps, but your heart is in the right place."

"Why, why did I take it upon myself to humiliate her so?"

"Because you are bored with confinement of winter, of your delicate condition, and I can see you are missing Frederick terribly. So it is only natural you should desire a happy and contented marriage for Beatrice, one in which B will not be parted from her dearly beloved."

"Is that what you think? You think me discontent with my lot?"

"I think discontent is a strong word. Though I am of mind the falling in love aspect of romance left you vulnerable to the reality of a soldier's lot. Blinded by love, the inevitability of inner loneliness all soldier's wives must suffer never entered your head. Such has now befallen you and it's very difficult to bear. Am I right?"

"How is it that you are so aware of the pitfalls of marriage and all that it entails?"

"At twenty-four years of age and still unwed, one could say I have been gifted ample time to observe the consequence of marriage from a safe distance. But of course, it could equally be said, and probably has been voiced quite often by young men of the *haut beau monde*, when and if they are of mind to my absence from society, '*who would marry the Beaumont gal, not I?*'."

Rose sniffled; brimmed tears now abated. "I no longer fancy a muffin, do you?"

The pull bell at the front entrance suddenly clanged throughout the hallway and Georgette's reply, "I think I shall survive until dinner."

A smile swept to Rose' face, though a clatter and bang in the hall proved most distracting and raised male voices in argument was somewhat disconcerting. Before either had risen from their seats, the door opened and there stood Adam Brockenbury: Ranulph at his elbow, his artist's easel in pieces. She could only surmise a mêlée between the

25

brothers had occurred, hence the manservant face grim and hovering at Ranulph's rear.

"So it is true. Well, well," said Adam Brockenbury, striding to centre room. "The lady hath returned." He bowed in manner most conceited, his voice snide in tone. "Tell me, Georgette, do you wish to entertain notion of a welcome back to the *haut ton*? If so, it can be arranged."

His slate blue eyes rolled over her from head to foot and back to face, and as of old a lecherous glint, his saturnine features as unforgiving mean as ever. His use of her first name thus unforgiveable. If he thought her heart was pounding in fear he was absolutely correct. She loathed and feared him, and thought him capable of almost anything, including murder.

"You must come to Abbeyfields for dinner." He laughed, not quite mockery but almost. "Ally yourself with Eliza and she will assure a joyous reunion with all your old friends and acquaintances. She seems to have them all in her pocket, though I cannot imagine how such popularity befell her. She has the face of disgruntled brood mare." He again bowed, slapped a glove to thigh. "Tomorrow at eight. I shall send the carriage for half-seven to collect you." He glanced at Rose. "You will accompany her ladyship, I presume? And young Miss Knightley?"

Rose it seemed had lost her tongue. Perchance Adam's indiscreet reference to disgruntled brood mare not only rude in its presentation, but a reminder of her desire to remain fairly incognito until a hoped for Frederick junior was safe in the cradle.

Before Adam turned, as he was wont to do and his arrogant self to stride away in triumph, she stepped in saving Rose from embarrassment of silence "I thank you for your invitation, but I have a prior engagement tomorrow evening."

His manner implied disbelief, his tone cutting. "I offer you a token of friendship and you choose to throw sand in my face." His stance became impatient, even a hint of momentary disquiet at his being sidelined. Nonetheless he rallied with spite and malevolence in eye. "Has exclusion from society taught you nothing?"

She braved up to him. "Where exclusion for some may seem like purgatory. For others it is often a blessing."

His face creased to a sardonic grin. "Dearest Georgette, with whomever and wherever your engagement, postpone it. Father is now gone, and your presence is most welcome at Abbeyfields." He once again turned to Rose, his stance dismissive. "I look forward to your company and that of your sister. Your father, too, if he so feels inclined."

"I cannot speak for my father, and in my present condition it is with regret that I must decline your invitation. I weary so easily these days, and take to my bed quite early of evening."

"Forgive me, Mrs. Davenport, I had not realised." He bowed, and even managed a pleasant smile. "May I extend congratulations to you and your husband?" Without awaiting response from Rose, he turned again, this time his face a deceptive mask of propriety and sociability. "In spite of everything, Georgette; now that I am lord and master in residence at Abbeyfields, I really would deem your company at dinner a gracious enhancement to the occasion." With that he turned, and addressed Ranulph. "Edwin has arranged for a funeral of Friday next. Unfortunately, or perhaps, fortunate in my case, given the militia are at present setting about with questions of everyone within the district and upsetting many in the process, I truly thank God I have an engagement at Blenheim on the Friday."

Ranulph looked aghast at his elder brother's declaration. "You mean to miss father's interment?"

"What pray does it matter whether I am there or not? He's dead, gone, and soon to be buried."

With that Adam bowed to all and left the room accompanied by Barrett, the manservant. Utter silence befell the room until Ranulph held aloft his broken easel, and said, "Can hate be more profound than destruction for the sake of?"

Rose drew breath, anger and compassion evident in her outburst, "Did he do that, on purpose?"

"It's what he does. Another canvas is a sorry mess as well."

"Dear, dear Ranulph, and Adam will be at Abbeyfields more often now, I shouldn't wonder. How will you manage? What of your paintings? Are they safe?"

"As safe as can be while Edwin is at home. He is the one person Adam has failed to get the upper hand with, and if not for Edwin, father's death might well have passed as nothing more than a hunting accident . . ."

"Not foul play, surely?" said Rose.

"Edwin is adamant it was murder, for the knife embedded in father's chest is, in itself, unusual. And prior to his death it was never known to be in his possession. The local Constable agreed the circumstance of what happened to be odd indeed, and promptly called out the militia to conduct duties on his behalf."

Most certainly scandal was brewing, Lord Brockenbury's murder would now undoubtedly be on the tip of every tongue in the neighbourhood if not already bandied from village to town and back again. *Was this really such a good time for her, Georgette, to venture out into society as Adam had suggested? Perhaps not, for what if people presumed her reappearance and a second tragic death at Abbeyfields was more than coincidental?* She might even find herself tagged a murderess, and despite Edwin, who would verify her innocence in no uncertain terms, nevertheless her name might again be tarnished.

"I am so sorry," she said, a gentle hand momentarily applied to Ranulph's cuff, "you must miss him, terribly."

His response came as a total surprise. "I barely knew him. His dogs were allowed at table alongside James, Adam and Edwin, whereas I, the beastly cripple, thus made to dine in my rooms. Father could not bear to have me near him, and Adam conveys the same disgust to imperfection. Edwin on the other hand, is constant in reminding me that although I am un-fortunate in posture my talent is Heaven sent. He claims Adam is the Devil's spawn, borne to prey on the weakness of others, whilst he, the lawyer is borne to uphold the law and prey on the sinners of this world. In truth Edwin has the mind of a genius. He recalls dates, times and events in sequence with absolute clarity. If anyone can unmask father's killer, be sure Edwin will see that person brought to justice and to the hangman's noose."

She shuddered at Ranulph's fate under Adam and their father's unjust treatment. Rose too looked quite concerned and was probably thinking much as she in regard to unspeakable behaviour toward B's love interest. The broken easel alone was testament to his elder brother's evil streak, and she could well imagine acts of violence meted to Ranulph or at least such threatened. She knew only too well how vile Adam could be.

Beatrice swept into the room looking decidedly beautiful in a ravishing deep green silk; her gown rustling as though her silk slippers were treading through crispy autumn leaves.

29

"Oh Ranulph, your horrid, horrid brother," exclaimed Beatrice. "Must he always be so brutal and wicked?" She surveyed the remnants of his easel. "Will a chair and large foot stool suffice? Barrett has said he will bring one to the drawing room and, a very old wooden chair from the kitchen."

"That would be grand," replied Ranulph, face alight with renewed joy at again able to indulge his talent as a portraitist. "Lucky for us Adam failed to notice the spare canvas left leaning against the wall or he might have put his boot to that as well."

Beatrice caught up his hand and led him away, and as soon as the pair stepped out of earshot Rose said, "Will you accept Adam's invitation, for I know you have no prior engagement."

"I cannot think it in my best interests to do so and will therefore decline by letter. How, though, am I to prove prior engagement when I have no one else in the district I can pay visit to? I would prefer for Adam to at least hear of my presence elsewhere, all in due course, even though I feel no obligation to politeness in his direction."

Rose pressed her hands to head. "Thinking cap on, um-um-ummm— But of course. I know, I know who you can pay visit to."

"Who and where?"

"Frederick's parents. They are only a short drive away and not that enamoured of the Brockenbury circle." Rose stood up. "Come, let us go to the study. I shall write a note to my dearest mother-in-law, whom you will love. She is so funny and of great wit. Oh but of course, you've met before." There was no arguing with Rose, when her heart was firmly set on helping out a friend in need. "And you, dear Georgette, shall write and inform Adam how sorry you are but you simply could not break your engagement with the kindest and dearest of persons." Rose laughed. "If nothing else, he will think you have a new beau."

As they made their way to the study, she asked, "Who is Eliza?"

"Eliza Datchett, the Brockenbury boys' cousin. I had thought her destined to be Adam's wife. Well, at least, Beatrice was given to understand it was so according to Ranulph, but he has said no more about it."

"I would not wish Adam on any woman."

"You might if you should ever encounter Eliza, but what I know of her can wait for another day," said Rose, whilst opening the door to the study. "We have letters to compose."

Four

The Cathedral City of Wells.

Georgette blessed their luck of good weather.

"What a lovely day?"

"Wonderful, and I swear I have not walked so far in ages," said Rose, reaching out her hand to assist in sliding comfortable to a park bench. "Who would have thought the weather could turn so glorious, so warm when last week the ground was frozen solid."

Inhaling deeply, sweet scent drifting across the meadows assailed Georgette. "Violets, can either of you smell violets, or is it my imagination?"

Beatrice sniffed the air. "Yes, I do, and I know where we shall find them if we are of mind to wander farther afield."

Rose too, inhaled. "Oh yes, of course, over by Park Woods. We found them there before, all along the verge of the bridleway. In fact, we could stroll that way back, though it can be a little muddy in places. We may have to dodge wheel ruts, and might well encounter the occasional farm wagon."

"Do you think you should, dear sister, in your condition?"

"Beatrice dearest, I am not an invalid," snapped Rose, regaining her feet after the briefest rest taken along the way. "I fully intend making it to the cathedral, along the cloisters and out through the west door. We shall then peruse the shops and take tea in the square at Flossie's tea room and back via Park Woods." She crooked her arm, for her companions to link with her. "Now, ever onward."

They marched off arm in arm abreast, laughing as they went, and giggling each time they had to negotiate their way in single file through kissing-gates. Though on one occasion Beatrice scrambled over a style, and soon they were circumnavigating the moat surrounding the Bishop's Palace. They periodically paused to lean over the low wall seeking evidence of minnows or just to admire the swans; the pair shadowing them all the way to the drawbridge.

The swans looked quite expectant of tasty morsels, but when no breadcrumbs were proffered the glorious birds exited the water a few yards to the fore, ambled past the drawbridge and plopped back into the water. They then whirled about a few times still hoping for due reward, and again with none forthcoming they sailed majestic to one of the gatehouses. There the male promptly tugged at a bell-rope situated next to a gatehouse window; and quite persistent in ringing the bell attached. It was but a short while of waiting, and then with the window flung wide a mobcap appeared, a jolly face of maid, and the swans received scraps of food.

Delighted by the spectacle, Georgette and her companions clapped in unison, a deep voice from behind quite taking them by surprise. Shocked they all spun round to see Edwin Brockenbury.

"Good day to you, ladies," said he, and suddenly as though conscious of having caught them unawares, added, "I fear I intrude, your ladyship."

"Not at all," said she, a smile, "though I confess you caused my heart to miss a beat. I quite thought you were Adam."

He removed his hat, bowed to all, his eyes passing one to another and then settling to hers in discerning manner. "He is here— in the cathedral, with Eliza." He smiled then, his hat casual to hand. "I confess to having felt more gooseberry than anything else, and therefore tendered my

34

excuses and arranged to meet up with them at Flossy's Tea House at three."

His smile disarming she could barely muster words in reply, and although wishing to at least extend sense of welcome a needling thought leapt to mind. She glanced at each of her companions in turn, and it occurred to her they were thinking much the same. "What a coincidence, we are all here, in Wells, today."

"True enough, but on my honour I had no notion you ladies were paying visit here."

Rose upped and said, "We happen to be staying at Dulcote for a few days. It's but a steady walk away. And your family, are staying nearby, too?"

His expression remained unreadable but his eyes revealed alarm, awareness perhaps to something that otherwise would have passed as inconsequential and now connected to their meeting so unexpectedly.

"Indeed we are to stay over for a few days." He replaced his top hat to head; gentle pressure applied to the top to secure its fit. "It was agreed, after father's interment, it would be good for us all to get away for a few days. Ranulph, unfortunately, had a fall, a quite bad fall, and—"

"A fall?" exclaimed Beatrice, hand to mouth in shock horror. "How bad was his fall?"

"Sufficient to prevent his coming to Wells, and I shall return to Abbeyfields tomorrow, despite his insistence he would be staying abed and I was not to worry unduly, but I do."

"How did he fall? Where did he fall?"

"Miss Knightley," said he, addressing Beatrice directly. "It is not the first time Ranulph has taken a tumble down the stairs, and I suppose, given his many bruises, bed is probably the best place for him." He smiled, tentative and somewhat subdued in voice. "Can I escort you ladies around the cathedral? I presume that is next on your agenda."

It was obvious Edwin knew nothing of Beatrice's affections for Ranulph, though the girl put him straight on that right away. "Not I, for I must return home as soon as possible."

Distress in her voice was apparent for she turned on her heels and marched off, and Rose said, "She will need comforting, for she is very fond of Ranulph."

"That I can see," said Edwin, a smile, "I had no idea the pair had feelings for each other."

Rose looked to her sister several yards distant, and smiled at Edwin. "It was nice to see you again, such a long time since we last met, but I have to go. Georgette do stay, you can catch up with us later."

Once again he hauled his hat from head and bowed in acceptance of Rose's need for flight, and as Rose walked off calling to Beatrice, he said, "And yourself, my Lady. Will you stay, or go?"

"I would love to stay if sure we could be alone to take in the sights, but I think encounter with Adam and your cousin is a surety. Besides, I ought really to go, more for Beatrice than any selfish attempt to evade your kin. She is clearly distressed, and it seems probable our stay at Dulcote will be shorter than anticipated."

"Then could I take it upon myself to escort you to Dulcote, or at least part way there? There is something of importance I would like to put before you, and would greatly appreciate your thoughts on the matter."

"Oh—How can I help, if at all?"

"Shall we?" He gestured for her to follow in Rose's and Beatrice's steps. "You see, I have of late pondered how a lady might conceal a knife upon her person, presupposing she has no pockets."

As they set off at a goodly stroll she glanced through the vast stone archway to the town's square; clearly awash with carriages and a tradesman's cart ambling past. The utter tranquillity of the enclosed green alongside the Bishop's Palace was absolute stark in contrast to that of the hustle and bustle of the town. They were now alone, both Rose and Beatrice yards ahead.

"A woman, you suspect a woman in the case of your father's murder?"

"Let me say it all becomes a matter of eliminating the obvious and seeking the less evident in respect of murder. Motivation is either that of need and greed resulting in robbery, and thus murder by accident or intention. There was no robbery in my father's case, therefore murder was wholly unnecessary." Edwin glanced at her, his smile that of reassurance she supposed. "In cases of revenge, which tend toward harboured grudge of some sort or other then murder might occur. But after extensive brain-storming and questions asked of many it was concluded no one bore a grudge toward my father sufficient to commit murder."

"But why, why has suspicion fallen to that of a woman?"

"The Constable and I set about our task in methodical order and eliminated all the possibilities— inclusive of any reported escapee from the local asylum and that of the gaols in the district. No such escapes have occurred and no escapees reported as still on the run from any previous break outs. Now I have not discussed my theory of what may well have occurred that day, but I have heard rumours of an argument between my father and Adam. The crux at issue, Adam mentioned a possible union between him and our cousin Eliza."

The noisy gush of water at the moat's sluice gate drowned all other sounds, and Georgette abstained from casting a question at him. But once they had reached the

37

first kissing-gate which led to the parks footpath, she paused, asked, "Am I allowed to know why talk of a marriage caused an argument?"

"Of course." He pushed the gate forward, she stepped inside, paused and as she in turn attempted to swing it back their hands met mid-swing. She was sure he remembered a prior incident of intimacy as well as she did, for his eyes implied such, his voice too. "I would not be here if you thought me incapable of discretion, dear lady."

"*Please*, Georgette. Call me Georgette."

He followed her through the gate and proffered his arm. In effect his friendly action afforded close contact, which was only socially acceptable for couples officially walking out together.

She nonetheless accepted his gesture, and, "Georgette," rolled off his tongue in a husky whisper, her kid-clad fingers soon wrapped beneath his gloved hand. "And a very pretty name, may I say?"

The sensuality of his touch, and the way in which mischief sparkled in his eyes there was no doubt his intentions implied more than merely gaining womanly opinion on matters of murder. "So what is it, if anything, that you wish to put before me?"

His face creased in a hearty-worthy grimace. "I see you expect the worst from men and afford us little leeway, so I will get right to the business side of this acquaintance." A gentle squeeze to her hand accompanied his honest if perceptive comment, and although said in good heart it stung a little. "What I am about to reveal is far from common knowledge at Monkton Abbeyfields, and I trust it will go no further, not even become talked of at Fenemore."

"In simple terms it will not be discussed," said she. "I would state such on my honour, but given my rumoured past, perhaps it is not the best example of one's status."

He smiled, and again applied a gentle squeeze to her fingers "I think you sorely underestimate peoples' regard for you, and sadly allowed one incident to mar your life unnecessarily. But that aside, and not wishing to drag unpleasant aspects of the past to the fore, let us proceed with my present dilemma. As it stands, the Constable, the farm bailiff and I were all present when the knife embedded in my father's chest needed to be removed for the benefit of his laying out."

"I see, and how can I help in this matter?"

"Well, as it happens the murderer used a switchblade, a com-mon enough device and useful for personal protection." He glanced at her then, their eyes meeting in earnest cogency. "After all, I sport a sword-cane when travelling in areas that I deem unsafe. "However, this particular switchblade is of French origin. It has a silver grip handle and forward motion of the blade as opposed to sideswipe mechanism."

"By that you mean the blade is instantly to the fore emulating that of a dagger, unlike those that unfold from the grip?"

"Precisely, and in this instance a lethal spring-loaded device, for its grip can rest against any intended victim without their suspecting a thing, until the blade is set in motion."

She shivered at the thought of an unsuspecting victim suddenly aware that a blade has pierced their flesh, and throes of death upon them. "But I cannot see where I am supposedly able to help in this matter."

"As a woman, where might you secrete such a device other than within a dainty reticule?"

Their eyes collided, hers in consternation, his imploring help, and all the while that same sweet scent of violets drifted across the meadow as before. "Is the grip of the weapon heavy or light?"

"Much like that of a silver tableware knife."

"Any pockets I have tend small indeed, and dainty reticules in my possession might well reveal a switchblade grip within. But then, a small ladies mirror can be weighty if silver-backed."

"Playing devil's advocate here, let us suppose the murder was planned. We both know freezing stilled conditions prevailed by nightfall, and yet, throughout the greater part of the journey we experienced the pleasures of a sunny day and good company, albeit a somewhat cutting northerly wind battered the coach."

Thankful he thought of her presence in the coach as good company, she rallied with a notion so profound it quite astonished her. "A muff, a muff," she exclaimed. "A lady could easily conceal a switchblade in a large muff. My personal preference would be that of fur muff for who would suspect villainy of a woman bedecked with fur?"

"True, but a lady with fur muff, treading across mudded fields? Besides, she would need to withdraw it, thus seen by her intended victim before the villainous deed could be enacted."

"Yes, I see what you mean." A second kissing-gate now before them they disengaged arms and each in turn made through it, and instinctively about to link arms again as before, she held back. "No, no, a muff is perfect. I think I know how a woman could have committed the sin."

"How so?" said he, removing his hat, as though perhaps she wished him to turn back, their walk at end, solution to his problem nigh.

She gripped his arm. "With my left hand on your right arm," said she, though a glint of amusement dancing in his eyes implied doubt at her suggestion as a plausible scenario, she nevertheless continued. "Now, imagine my right hand is shrouded with a fur muff. Could I not easily lay it to your chest, and release the blade?"

A smile swept to his face. "If we were lovers then I would agree, for if I leaned forward to kiss you," which he implemented with surprising accomplishment, and his voice a husky whisper on retreat was soul destroying: "You could at this very moment commit murder."

She stepped back, a silly girlish flush to her cheeks and yet burning desire to enact that same delightful kissing scenario over and over again. "I concede to your knowledge all things lovers. Unfortunately our quest to discover how a woman might approach a man with murder in mind is now no closer than before."

"Then let us try another scenario in which I make the first move."

In itself his movement proved earnest with intent, his arm about her waist vicelike and her body crushed to his meaningful. The kiss too, proved far more potent in delivery than his prior brief brushing of her lips. Unlike someone intent on murder she succumbed and allowed him full invasive possession. Delighting in his ardent if somewhat inappropriate advance, she despaired the moment of his pulling back, and when it came, her heart fell flat, but she mustered air of disquiet, "I feel somewhat duped in this strange matter of your dilemma."

His smile disarming, he said, "But Georgette, you are, supposedly a murderess most foul and the deed yet to be done." He plonked his hat to head, and infuriatingly gave it a pat on top. "I admit most shamefully in taking advantage of your vulnerability in a most outlandish manner." Without further preamble he drew her hand to his lips, sufficient to cause her heart to blip, as he further said, "To beg forgiveness in this unseemly matter would be churlish, but I will say my admiration for the lady who shared her coach with me knows no bounds."

"Consider yourself forgiven, Edwin, for I cannot be excused for my part in what occurred between us." She shot him a smile, reached for his arm, and stepped in beside him. "Should I take your action to mean we are now walking out, or are we once again characters in a travesty of murder, and intent only on exploring all the possibilities of a murderess at work?"

"Of the former mentioned I am delighted to oblige as often as you feel fit to give me leave to fulfil my heart's desire, and of the latter I am truly grateful for your help."

She laughed and hugged his arm to her breast. "I confess to great appreciation of our journey from London, for when you fell asleep it afforded time for much consideration of your handsomeness. And I did, in all honesty, fantasise a little on the prospect of our meeting up again— On a more intimate and social basis, until of course, the accident and your destination then revealed."

"Ah yes, not as I had planned. Fear of recognition reflected in your beautiful green eyes revealed far more than words could ever have conveyed at that moment when my name became known to you."

"Did you know Adam invited the Knightleys' and me to dinner of Wednesday last? We declined, due to a prior engagement?"

"No, I had no knowledge whatsoever of a dinner engagement, but I now know why he was in such a foul mood and why he left for Blenheim before dinner that night." He glanced her way, his grey eyes saying so much in silent caress words were unnecessary. "It would have pleased me had you accepted the invitation." He sighed, as though despairing of events in the past two weeks. "Any grief at father's passing has lain for the most part on my shoulders, for he and Adam had not a good word to say one to, or about the other. As for Ranulph, no love loss there, and I feel sure you have been made aware of his fate at Monkton Abbeyfields when but a child. The Knightley girls could not help but be aware of Ranulph's unhappy upbringing, for father literally abandoned him to the servants to rear and cater for his needs. The poor fellow, afflicted with rickets, suffered terribly and never a moment of compassion extended his way by father."

"I have heard tell a little of his suffering, and witnessed for myself Adam's abysmal behaviour toward him, which did cause me to ponder the sort of ungodly treatment Ranulph might at any time be subjected to, if Adam was ever in need of venting spleen."

"Witnessed, when?"

"At Fenemore. Adam stormed into the house, smashed your brother's easel and put his foot through a canvas. Poor Ranulph had come there purposefully to prep the beginnings of a portrait of Beatrice."

"Dear God, in the Knightley's house? Whatever possessed Adam?" He slipped her arm from his, and turned to face her. "What exactly have you heard, about Ranulph? You see, I am rarely at home these days so am quite out of the goings on at Abbeyfields."

She sensed him angered, wary and half dreading her reply. "I can only repeat what I've heard and cannot verify any of it, other than I think Ranulph is utterly delightful company." A reassuring smile escaped her for Ranulph's happy face at the tea table remained memorable. "You and I both know the Knightleys' are far from given to fanciful imaginings of brutality, but Beatrice has mentioned cases of unexplained bruises on Ranulph's face and unaccountable bouts of pain. All, I might add, believed unrelated to his

43

physical deformity. His excuses for his injuries have ranged from tripping over stools, to bumping into chairs and falling down the stairs."

"And you think Adam might be responsible for the injuries sustained by Ranulph?"

"I think him more than capable of merciless cruelty. In fact, on the night of James' death, certain aspects of what occurred I could not for the life of me remember when asked over and over at the time. And it became impossible to think clearly, and everything that happened became akin to a jumbled jigsaw puzzle in my head. But in recent weeks little pieces of the jigsaw have come to light, and I feel as though the puzzle is now half done with, and what I see troubles me."

"What do you see, Georgette? Please, what is it that troubles you about that night? As you know, or might remember, I was not in attendance at the summer ball, so I have nothing but recollections by others as to the sequence of events leading up to James' unholy death. To date, little of what occurred two years ago has ever made sense to me."

"Nor I, for I hardly knew James. I barely knew Adam despite my being there at your father's invitation. And I swear I had no knowledge of your elder brother's dark side until that very night. Of course, already friends with the Knightley girls we soon linked up, and there were lots of other people I knew quite well, or thought I did until what happened and no one wanting any association with me thereafter."

"Come, let us sit awhile," said he, in kindly manner, a park bench at one pace distant. "Perhaps it would be better to discuss this another time, another place maybe? For I sense you are somewhat distressed by memories of that dreadful night."

She settled to the park bench. "I am upset, not so much for me but for you."

He settled beside her. "Why for?"

"First your brother killed, then your father, and now—"

"*Killed*? James murdered? What made you say killed?" Eyes locked she saw realisation slowly dawning. "Dear God, so you think foul play?"

"I cannot say for sure. I cannot find those pieces. What I see when I concentrate my mind is Adam storming off toward James who is so drunk he can barely stand upright, and I think Adam has a pistol in his hand. But you see, restrained by one of Adam's friends and trying to fend him off, I cannot be sure it is a pistol, nor whence it came into Adam's hand. A second man steps into the fray and between them they force me back inside the coach house, then a pistol is fired."

"And?"

Tears spilled forth, memories raw, as a handkerchief was duly handed over. Edwin's eyes so full of compassion and empathy, she felt obligated to recall finite details of that dark and miserable night. Her downfall from grace seemed immaterial alongside murder, which in all probability had occurred that night.

"As much as I wish to hear your account of what happened, if you feel unable to continue I will understand and desist in putting forth questions."

She sniffled, the handkerchief welcome, so too his hand laid to hers. She closed her eyes, the scene of that awful night once again upon her.

"Take a deep breath, Georgette, and piece by piece we may solve this particular mystery, yet."

Drawing breath she let that awful, awful night wash over her. "Upon the sound of the pistol fired, the men are as though turned to stone, and I at liberty to escape, which I do

45

but only to run into Adam. I see James in the stable yard in a crumpled heap. Adam is bending over him. Oh God, I want to know what has happened, but Adam stands up and hauls me back to the coach house. He shouts to his friends, '*get outside, and keep your mouths shut or else*'. I distinctly remember his exact words, and I think he told them to say they found James with a pistol in his hand. Adam then tells me to '*hide in the hayloft*'. I remember that part too, and he further said, '*you must not be seen in the stable yard with so many young men in attendance, or your name will be mud, Georgette*'. Foolishly I did as he said, and he helped to haul me aloft and that's when he tried to. Oh God, I can't go on, I can't."

Edwin's arm wrapping about her shoulder in a comforting manner, at any other time a thoroughly delightful prospect, but it was even more welcome in its present form.

"It's all right, it's all right, Georgette, shed your tears, let the pain flow."

She sniffled, continued, "Luckily Adam never succeeded in his attempted rape that night, because all hell broke loose and to some extent saved me from that most awful of fates."

Edwin's tight embrace conveyed relief at news of her escape from Adam's clutches. Though she sensed something else too, which was not so unexpected for it meant she was not, as imagined, sullied goods, yet his words implied him innocent of such thoughts.

"The more I learn of Adam's brutal treatment of others the more I think him capable of murder."

"To be honest my saviour that night was the head groom, for roused by the pistol shot he rallied the stable hands. As the lads tumbled out of their quarters opposite to the stable loft, the head groom spied Adam and I. Thence my disgrace was made known to all below in the stable yard by your hateful brother. A throng had gathered and Adam played as though to an audience. While I protested my innocence he branded me a trollop and declared me as the cause of James' death."

"Believe me, Georgette, when I say, I believed my brother's death was genuine suicide due to a few unpaid debts, and nothing whatsoever to do with you. Yet later, I discovered James' debts were nowhere near as vast as accrued by Adam. I do need to rethink that night of the summer ball, and re-evaluate father's death and seek foul play afoot in a way I had not envisaged beforehand."

"Do you still think a woman might be involved?"

"It was a line of investigation and of much speculation." His gaze wandered across the meadows but momentary and once again levelled on hers. "All that I now know makes my earlier assumptions less valuable, and perhaps motivation for murder is of a very different nature than first thought. Hmmm. Love and sense of vengeance might well have had a part to play in James' death, but with father's death there is now nothing in the way to prevent something desired when previously denied to that person."

"It all sounds very complicated, and do be careful Edwin, for I sense danger close at hand. Given what I know, and what I think has happened to Ranulph."

"What gain could there be if I died this night?" said he, a reassuring hug applied to her person. "I am neither heir to my father's estate nor Ranulph for that matter, but surprising as it may seem, father did provide for Ranulph in the form of a small property in Bath"

"Nevertheless, you remain a threat Edwin, a serious threat to any person who might think you are close to uncloaking the truth behind James' death. I beg of you, cease your involvement and let the Constable take it upon his shoulders to bring the culprits to justice."

"Am I to understand you care for my reckless lawyer hide?" His smile tugged at her heartstrings, her hand again lifted to his lips as tortuous as were his words: "Though such, if true, would please me greatly."

"Then heed my warning, for whom else can I walk out with if not the man I most admire?"

"Shall I walk on with you, or would you prefer I retreat and leave you in peace?"

"Come with me to the last gate, it is but another meadow away. And the house where I am staying is a mere short walk from there."

Quick to feet, he said, "In that case I shall see you to the door, and depart all the happier knowing you are safe in the company of friends." Heart racing, she accepted the hand proffered by her new beau, for that's what he had become, and much to her delight.

Five

Why a missive?

Edwin had as good as said he would be on his way to Abbeyfields by eight of morn, and now his promise to Beatrice was already broken. The curt note, delivered early that very morning by private messenger was quite unexpected. His request for Lady Georgette Beaumont to meet with him most urgent in the cathedral's *Chapter House* at precisely eleven of morning, equally disturbing. After all, *Georgette* had rolled off his tongue the day before in a manner most affectionate.

Quite taken aback at the message itself worded more command rather than polite request. Thus, in like to Rose, she thought it rather odd and a little disconcerting, for it seemed so out of character for Edwin. Nevertheless, the note implied urgency, and the head groom aware of her plight had kept the horses at a goodly trot to get her to town by eleven.

Whilst ascending the *Chapter House* steps the clock began striking eleventh hour and each strike reverberated beneath her feet. It was a strange sensation indeed, as though the steps were rocking to and fro. The acoustics inside *The Chapter House* such that a pin dropped was likened to a hammer blow, as discovered when her reticule slipped from trembling fingers; a gentle if amplified whooshing sound all about her whilst it slid across the floor.

On retrieving her silk reticule she glanced upward, the window lights ablaze with sunshine. Whether the ornate fan effect of vaulted ceiling and sheer height of the central pillar towering upward, or the sound of heavy footfalls on the steps, she nonetheless felt quite light-headed and stumbled backwards.

Caught mid-stumble, it was Edwin she expected to be her rescuer not Adam. "*You*," she exclaimed in hushed whisper, though her word thus amplified as though shouted to the heavens.

"Dearest Georgette—I trust you are not hurt." Adam released her from his grasp, and bowed. "My Lady," thus purred forth with a possessive bent, "you seem a little upset that I should happen upon you." He smiled; his face a picture of triumphant glory. "Needless to say, I knew you would be here."

"So it was you who sent the note?"

"I confess to element of deception, yes, but I fear you and I have drifted apart, and much to my chagrin the fault is all mine. Nevertheless, the ties that bind us are tight indeed."

"Bind us? We barely knew each other two years ago, and know little of one another now."

"I beg to differ, for you know of my strengths and weaknesses, Georgette, and the latter once yourself. Did I not call most regular at your father's London address? I know full well the curt response to the effect, *'the lady Georgette is not available'* came as instruction from your sweet lips."

"I had it in mind your weakness for female company extended only to that of becoming master of womanly flesh, rather than any motive to woo such to your arms."

He thrust his hand to chest as though mortally wounded by cut and thrust of blade to his heart as opposed to her tongue cutting him to verbal shreds. "I deserve that blow and more, but come, Georgette, of all the women I've had, not one has matched the ferocity of your tongue. Nor has any one of them fought as you fought that night of the summer ball."

Fear and dread gripped her. Adam had not sent word to lure her here to talk of untold desires and at how his heart was broken, he was here to inflict misery and to remind her of what had happened that dreadful night, and how it was nothing compared to what might happen if ever she let slip a word of his part in James' death. That or he hoped she was too traumatised by it all to remember clearly what had transpired on that ungodly night. He could so easily see her as a threat if he now knew she and Edwin were walking out. For her sake and Edwin's it was best to impart no memory of that night beyond the incident in the hayloft.

"I simply do not understand you at all. Your brother committed suicide that night, and you Adam, thought of nothing but having your way with me."

"*Georgette*," said he, exasperation evident in tone and thoughtless need to inner frustrations, "I was mad for you. Mad in wanting to make love to you."

"Love? You think to rape is to make love?"

"I thought your putting forth resistance was little more than heightening the thrill of the moment. Damn it all, you fought like a wild cat. Even when I kissed you as gentle as able, still you put forth resistance."

"I was scared Adam, terrified of what you were about, and I knew it all meant nothing to you. Once gratification was achieved you would have walked away without a backward glance."

He reached for her hand.

She recoiled.

"Oh Georgette, Georgette. Believe me, you stole my heart that memorable day in London, and that is why you were invited to the ball. I purposefully asked father to extend invite yourself and your grandfather, which would not have happened otherwise. Of a parochial mindset, father hated every hour spent in the House of Lords and thought only of close friends and notable families whom he felt comfortable with. When your acceptance arrived, it gladdened my heart, and I thought only of the glorious time I would derive from escorting you around the ballroom, but you took it upon yourself to flirt with James, and infatuated by you he stole virtually every dance."

"I barely knew him, but will say he was one of the most enchanting men I'd had the good fortune to meet that night. Quick-witted and of good humour he made me laugh, and yes I liked him well enough, but when Rantchester and the others dragged him away in boisterous and jolly manner, I thought no more about him. I danced two dances with you, if I recall correctly, and we partook of refreshments long before James chose to reappear."

"Disgracefully drunk at that, and his proposal of marriage was outrageous, yet you played along with him and let him lead you off to the garden and thence to the stable yard. It was out of order, and yes, I poked fun at him. The fool was so enamoured by you and on his knees begging you to marry him, I had to do something, and do I did and rid you of a gross problem."

Dear God, he was as good as confessing to murder.

"I cannot recall any proposal of marriage," she lied, "all I remember is you atop me and your hands all about me in vile manner. And when I tried to fight you off, you sideswiped me with the back of your hand."

"Damn it all, Georgette. I was madly in love with you. I needed and wanted you to be mine."

He stepped closer and she could not move, simply could not move. Fear held her fast in its grip, the memory of his touch vile, but because of where they were sense of strength washed over her. She would see this through to its bitter end, for no happy conclusion could result from this meeting.

"Georgette, *Georgette*," he said, emitting a sigh. "I shall have you know I did fall in love with you that day in Hyde Park, and to this day I recall the gown you were wearing. It was pale blue with lemon ribbon trim, and you were the most exquisite woman I had ever set eyes upon."

She could vaguely remember that day, but it was nothing more than insignificant moment of his riding by, and his reining-about as men were wont in making a lady's acquaintance. "It matters not Adam, for that day in London is far behind us, and I remember your approach as somewhat pointed as though you thought my friends and I were girls from a theatre troupe."

He chuckled, amused in extreme. "At first, perhaps, but when you spoke I knew then my mistake, and did I not treat you with the utmost respect thereafter?"

"You did, I grant you that much, and poor Beatrice became infatuated with you on that day. And for all your talk of undying love for me, why then did you take advantage of her innocence on the night of the summer ball?"

"Spite, sheer spite, for I bargained a little flirting with the girl would rouse jealousy within you, and I quite thought my ruse had worked its magic when Rantchester danced you close to the terrace doors. For when you spied Beatrice and I, how shall I say, somewhat intimate, you flew at me and wrenched the stupid girl from my clutches." He laughed. "How well I remember your catlike glare and sharpness of tongue tearing me to shreds, and had it all happened in the ballroom instead of on the terrace, a hullabaloo might have kicked off. As it turned out, and as I remember, you said not a word of what had happened should pass beyond those present in attendance. To which both I and Rantchester agreed."

"Beatrice was but a romantic-minded child, barely sixteen, and you a man of the world. She thought of you as her prince, her hero, and I dare say she might well have succumbed to anything you had asked of her."

"Indeed, but the throb in my groin was of your doing not hers. Now do you see why I needed you, and how much I wish to make amends for what I did, to you, to our friendship? Thoughts of you, Georgette, drive me insane, to such an extent I make life for others hell on this earth."

She dearly prayed she would not choke on the partial lie she was about to put forth in the house of God. "Then let us both make amends here and now." She drew breath, heart palpitating. "I forgive you your indiscretion, and shall again think of you as a kindly acquaintance and friend in the making."

He snatched at her hand, and drew it to his lips. "Dearest Georgette, please, I beg of you, come to Monkton Abbeyfields for the spring ball. For only you can make of me a man who will gladden your heart, and I promise, on my life— you shall have me body and soul. I shall be your servant to command, as you see fit."

Astonished at his proclamation of love and declaration to become a changed man at her instigation, she half expected a flash of lightning and thunderbolt to smite the pair of them: liars both.

She snatched her hand away and fled; *The Chapter Steps* lethal when fearing God's wrath and sure the Devil was on one's heels. Halfway down the steps she passed a woman standing quite motionless. From the description Rose had proffered, the haughty persona and scowling face had to be none other than that of Eliza Datchett. The poor thing could not have failed to hear what had come to pass in *The*

Chapter House, despite much of it voiced in hushed whispers. If not for Edwin's theory of a murderess at large she would have afforded sympathy toward the Datchett girl, but if looks were anything to judge by, Eliza Datchett might have thrust a dagger to her heart: if given the chance.

Already in flight it would have been foolhardy to stop and indulge small talk, besides it seemed Adam would be hard-pressed to explain himself and placate his cousin, the would-be-bride and next Lady Brockenbury.

She shivered; the ultra cool interior of the cathedral a stark reminder of where she was, and a moment of prayer or meditation was utterly inadvisable. She hurried to the cloisters, which led to the Bishop's Palace. Nothing could help her now in calming her racing heart and galloping pulse. This was the safest and swiftest access to the town square. Adam would expect her to depart by way of the north door the same as entered beforehand, and had no doubt watched from a shadowed corner to be sure she had indeed abided to his dictate.

Glad to once again be outside in sunshine, and with no one in sight she took it upon herself to run the few yards to the grand archway. As soon as reached she spied her modest carriage and two-in-hand no more than a few paces distant. Young Turner, alert and earnest in his position as head groom and driver of the carriage, he spied her on approach and acquired a lad hovering nearby to take hold of the lead horse. After all, it was Turner's job to see her safely aboard, comfortable and the carriage door secure before setting off.

She waited whilst he thanked the lad with a farthing tossed into the air, but as Turner clambered aboard she asked, "Would it be possible to return to Dulcote a different way than that by which we came to town?"

"Tis mor'n possible yer ladyship, if you is happy to take a bit of rough with smooth." He smiled then, a beaming smile upon his ruddy face. "If you do get my meaning, fer the bridleway be a pretty ride."

"Then we shall take the pretty ride, and bear the rough with the smooth." Thank heaven for bridleways, for Adam would expect her carriage to take to the highway and might even attempt to follow in his own carriage. "Do not spare the horses, Turner, and let us fly home."

The laughter that drifted back as they set off was cheering indeed, for Turner had taken her jest in good heart. "Aye m'lady."

He was home, and ran up the grand staircase and hastened along the upper corridor to the west wing, where Ranulph had his own rooms. He knocked the outer door, Ranulph's voice loud and clear in reply:

"Entrée, Jenkins."

He laughed, for Ranulph's manservant had already informed him he would find his brother with paints to canvas, though still a little stiff in limb and only able to stay on his feet for short spells of exercise.

"Edwin," exclaimed Ranulph, delight etched upon his face. "Back so soon?"

"I have my reasons, and one being Beatrice Knightley."

"Why, has something happened? Is Beatrice all right?" Despair in his eyes Ranulph hurriedly laid his palette aside and thrust his brush to pot, and with some difficulty struggled to sit in a chair. "Tell me, tell me about Beatrice."

"I am back because young Beatrice is worried about you."

"Me?"

"She has it in her head your tumble down the stairs was no accident."

"But it was."

"Was it?" Ranulph's flushed cheeks confirmed Beatrice Knightley's suspicions that he was nowhere near as clumsy as he made himself out to be. "The truth Ranulph, I want nothing but the truth from you. Now, did you fall or were you pushed?"

Ranulph closed his eyes and let fall his head, as though in shame. "I shall be leaving here in a day or two, and whether I fell or not is of little consequence. Jenkins is to come with me, for it was his wish to remain in my service, and Adam has agreed to it and that is all there is to be said on the matter."

"You have a gem of a girl in Miss Beatrice Knightley, and I hope you know how lucky you are."

"I do, but what right have I, a cripple, to ask for her hand in marriage?

"You love her and she loves you. That is blatantly obvious even to me. Besides, you now have your own house. You have modest means readily to hand, and substantive monies bequeathed and soon to be in the bank in your name. At least sufficient income for the present, and to see you stocked with paints and canvas in order to paint every damn lady of the *ton* hereabouts, not to mention those of the *haut monde* whom flock to Bath for the Season."

Ranulph's face came alight with brotherly enthusiasm cast his way. "You think, really think I could become a sought after portraitist?"

"Good lord, even I'm tempted to sit for you, though cannot for the life of me think where in the deuce I could hang a portrait of myself."

Ranulph struggled to his feet and walked awkwardly to a

canvas laid face to the wall. He turned it around. "Where would you hang this, if it was yours?"

"When did you do this?"

"Last week, whilst her ladyship's face remained fresh in my memory— B's portrait, sadly, lies unfinished and at Fenemore, so I thought why not, why not capture the Lady Georgette's beauty, as I see it."

"Beautiful indeed." A frisson of pleasure rippled down Edwin's spine, for it was as though Georgette was there, in the room. "Will you present it to her?"

"I can hardly gift it to her, can I, not as I shall with B's portrait."

"Then what. Sell it to her?"

"No. I think it has to be one of several portraits that will never see light of day."

Edwin wanted the portrait, wanted to purchase it. The thought of it hidden from view was unbearable but as yet, Adam nor Ranulph knew of his keened regard for Georgette, and for the time being it was best such news remained secret.

"There is another reason for my swift return to Abbeyfields." He drew breath, not the easiest of tasks before him, but questions needed answers. "The night of James' death, you were here in your rooms all day and all night. But did you, at any time see or hear what happened in the stable yard?"

Ranulph shifted in his chair, sense of unease about him and wary with it. "Why ask that of me now, when I told father and you I saw nothing, nothing at all."

"I have reason enough to believe James' death was that of murder, not suicide."

"Wwww—why? Whaaa—t— reason?"

He had not heard Ranulph stutter in a long while, and truth might well have remained buried forever by induced fear of retribution, but questions would be answered even if it took all day and all night to reassure Ranulph that he, Edwin, would protect him from Adam's detestable scorn and violence. "Jealousy, insane jealousy, is what I see as motive enough, though ascendancy as father's direct heir cannot be dismissed lightly, either."

"I saw nothing, I tell you, n n n n nothing."

"Your windows overlook the stable yard, and I know you said you were asleep and heard nothing, but I think you did. I think you heard voices, and like any curious person you went to a window to look out and see for yourself what was happening below. Is that not correct, Ranulph? You saw what happened and, perhaps, who knows, guilt at what he had done caused Adam to glance up at your windows. Is that what happened? Did Adam see you?"

Tears brimmed in Ranulph's eyes, the truth untold before and now rushing out in a torrent of hatred and dread of their elder brother's wrath. "His brother, his own brother and Adam treated him no better than a lame horse. I saw, yes I saw what happened, for I awoke to shouts of despicable utterances, and when I reached the window Adam was standing before James. I knew then Adam had hit him, for James could barely stand and he was leaning against the wall for support. I watched him slide to the ground, and Adam—Oh God, God forgive my sinful cowardice." Ranulph's shoulders began to shake, shudders strafing his frame and tears rolling down his face.

"It's all right, Ranulph. Tell me all, and I promise on my honour justice will be brought to bear upon Adam."

"I saw him, saw him standing over James, and then a pistol shot rang out. He has always said I am not your brother, not James, not his. He will kill me if ever it be known I have told you all this. He despises me. He thinks me no better than a cur to be kicked at will. He as good as

59

claimed mother had duly begotten just punishment for adultery with another man. That her giving birth to me, the cripple, was her undoing."

"That is a lie, a wicked lie." Edwin strode across to Ranulph, a hand to shoulder in heartfelt commiseration. "I shall forever remember her as a loving mother." A lump rose to his throat, memories unbearable leaping to mind. "Dear God, I so remember a nightmare moment of her fending off Adam when it became apparent she was again with child. He went berserk. He screamed at her. Kicked at her legs, and thumped her in the stomach. Father was out at the time and it took all our strength, James and I, to haul him away from her. She told father what had happened and it was decided it was high time for Adam to go away to school, but they chose to send him farther away than James and I. He went to Winchester, and we were at Westminster where mother had opportunity enough to see us when she and father were at our London house. Of course she saw Adam only for the duration of the school holidays."

"She didn't fall down the stairs, did she, any more that I do? She was pushed. That's what killed her, Edwin, is that not so?"

"If you are telling me Adam has pushed you down the staircase, and that he sets about you with his fists, then I think it is more that possible Adam did assist with mother's fall. How else would a perfectly fit woman tumble to her death down that staircase out there? He was at home as were James and I, for it happened the week of Christ's mass and you were but a poor little mite. She truly grieved your confinement up here and begged father to allow you to attend at table, but he would have none of '*her bleating*' as he called it. That's why James and I always sneaked up to your rooms by way of the servant stairs. That. or our lives would have been the worse if caught, but we never were."

60

"Coward that I am I stay in my rooms or go to Fenemore when Adam is in residence here. I thought I had succeeded well in avoiding him this visit, until the morning he came up here asking after Lady Beaumont. He was so sure she was at Fenemore. I rightly said I had not seen her there. At the time I did not even know she was in Batheaston. Then, that very afternoon I went to Fenemore and whilst there Adam arrived. He called me a lying toad, and in a terrible rage smashed my easel and put his foot through a canvas. He then accosted Lady Georgette, one minute vile in temper the next becalmed and moderate in manner. I thought her brave in facing up to him, but throughout I sensed she feared him greatly."

"She does, and what has passed between us here today must go no further. You do understand?"

"Of course I do, and would greatly appreciate your help in getting me out of this house and into my own as soon as possible."

"Then so be it. I shall have a cart brought to the house and between Jenkins and I and the upper household staff, we shall have you out of here before nightfall on the morrow."

Six

Time flew, and all were safe and back at Fenemore for all of four days; thus Georgette's stay was extended by persuasive influence of the Knightley sisters. Besides, a letter from Ranulph to Beatrice had drawn forth much excitement, and with the carriage ordered out front at two of afternoon they had, by invitation, set off to pay visit at his new house in Brock Street.

The house, upon approach, seemed most suitable for Ranulph's future occupation as a portraitist.

Ladies of high fashion were already noted as having ordered their modes of equipage to slowdown on passing No 14, their eyes drawn to the windows on the ground floor, as on this very day.

"What are they looking at?" exclaimed Beatrice, "what can they be looking at?"

Rose tittered, as the carriage drew closer, for there stood a portrait to easel and placed centre window. "How opportune the house should lie on the shaded side of the street," said she. "One could be quite forgiven for thinking the almighty had a hand in the placing of this house and of Ranulph's inheriting it."

"Oh my goodness, do you know that woman, Georgette? Do you know her?" enquired Beatrice, as though expecting a miracle from a once lady of the *haut ton*.

She had not thought it would be too long before ladies of Bath would be alighting from grand carriages in haste to see their reflections forever captured on canvas, but this lady's face quite escaped her. Besides, Ranulph had only taken up

63

residence a few days beforehand. Therefore the commission would have been undertaken some time ago.

"I have no idea, B."

As their carriage came to a standstill Rose gave the portrait much consideration, and finally said, "Do you not see family resemblance, for the lady is not so unalike Ranulph."

"Her hair, yes," said Beatrice fair leaping from the carriage, not taking heed of a gentleman passing by whom offered his assistance and promptly opened the carriage door for her. He smiled at Beatrice as though half expecting some sort of response, but no, for Beatrice' eyes had settled on the portrait, again. "You are so right, Rose. She has his beautiful blue eyes."

"Let me," said Georgette, stepping forth to alight ahead of Rose; the gentleman's hand accepted with due grace. "Thank you, so very much."

He tipped his hat, bowed, cast a smile, "Lady Georgette, my pleasure," and then carried on his way toward *The Royal Crescent*.

Although aware of past acquaintance she could not recall introduction to the extremely well-dressed gentleman. But it did seem young men of the *beau monde*, and his manners and dress suggested him a man of good fortune, had not forgotten her. She quickly turned and held out her hand to Rose. "Take care, now, it's quite a step down."

Rose laughed. "Oh Georgette, what would I do without you to guide my toes where I can no longer see."

Georgette laughed, too. "Not for much longer. Soon your soldier boy will be nestled to a cradle and you again as svelte as ever."

"I see you have acquaintance with yon gentlemen soldier, again."

"Soldier?"

"Not in uniform I grant you, and none other than the Marquis of Rantchester."

She glanced after the gentleman striding onward at a goodly pace, tipping his hat to ladies passing him by in their carriages.

"Oh, but of course." Dear heaven, she remembered now, remembered the last time she had set eyes upon him. How could she forget, forget the Marquis of Rantchester so readily, when it was he who had held her in restraint the night of James Brockenbury's death? "How strange that I should forget him?" she said aloud, and quite unintentional.

"Perhaps if astride a horse you might have recalled him more easily."

"True, but I have been absent from society for two years, and cannot be expected to remember every aristocrat met along life's path."

"Upon my soul," gasped Rose, feigning hurt, "the sharpness of your tongue today. Do I perceive element of abrasion at your meeting with him a moment past?"

How lucky for Rantchester, despite his handsomeness, that she had rendered him invisible to memory, his presence in the stable yard the night of James death recalled in name only.

"Dear Rose, forgive me, it is nonsense to feel so nervous after my outings to Wells, except that I am at this very moment stepping out where I have not stepped in two long years. For the City of Bath is the hub of the Wessex *ton*, and I risked exposure and rebuttal and looks of scorn whilst riding along in the carriage."

"But none of that did we encounter along the way. If anything, people have acknowledged you with smiles and gracious nods of heads, more so than that extended to Beatrice and I. And the Marquis could not have been more pointed in his stopping to assist in your alighting from the carriage. I am no fool, and if truth be told, he purposefully stopped to assist *you,* not Beatrice."

"Cease your silly dispute," snapped Beatrice tugging at a bell-pull. "It is neither the time nor the place for petty squabbles as to whether a marquis stopped simply to engage with Georgette or not."

Rose burst into laughter and wrinkled her nose. "I do declare you sound somewhat miffed, Miss Cross-Patch. Perchance you favoured the cut of the Marquis' swagger after all."

"Not I, for I know of his reputation well enough." Beatrice glanced in the direction of *The Royal Crescent*, the marquis nowhere in sight. "Where did he vanish to? He was there a moment ago, standing near to the end house."

They followed her gaze, Rose quick to say, "Oh, so his swagger did catch your eye."

"Only in so much as I thought him loitering in strange manner, his eye this way."

Before another word was uttered by any one of them the door to No 14 flew open and there stood Jenkins. "The master awaits in his upper rooms."

Jenkins stepped back allowing entry, and it then became apparent as to how cosy the interior was, for they entered into a small salon with staircase to upper floor; the walls draped with Ranulph's artwork.

Quick with eye Georgette noted the hallway carried onward traversing front to rear and a garden door at the end. Presumably the room with the portrait at its window lay to their left.

Upon Jenkins announcing their presence, it was Edwin who stepped forth from the room, the door left wide and two windows noted, the room itself though modest in size most elegant and a comfortable enough reception room.

"Jenkins, please be good enough to show Mrs. Davenport and Miss Knightley to Mr. Ranulph's sitting room." He bowed to Rose and Beatrice, his eyes then settled on hers. "Would you mind, Lady Georgette?" he said most formal, gesturing her toward the portrait room. "I have news from London."

Beatrice and Rose followed Jenkins up the staircase, Beatrice evidently in thrall and wonder and voicing much approval of portraits and landscapes.

Georgette, meanwhile, left in Edwin's company, they entered the portrait room, which felt akin to folly but she nonetheless stepped inside heart and pulse at odds.

Edwin closed the door, and although socially unacceptable for them to be alone in a room with the door closed, it mattered not, not even when Edwin caught her elbow, spun her round and drew her into his arm. The embrace on its own was breathtaking, while the kiss was pure ecstasy.

"Do you have any idea of the torture inflicted upon my heart when I spied Rantchester out there, knowing what I know about him and the part he played in your fate at Adam's hands?" He let slip his hold upon her, stepped back, and she wished he had not, but he furthered with, "I wanted to step outside and throttle the bounder."

"I confess I failed to recognise him at all, not even when he referred to me by name. It was Rose's teasing about his kindly action, and his name brought forth in jest that sent a chill of realisation down my spine."

"Men like Rantchester, and their misguided belief a gentleman's word must be honoured, may hold sway on silence to a murder committed but conscience will nonetheless sit heavy on their shoulders."

He looked at her then, his grey eyes expressing something deep. Perhaps his quest to unravel a tapestry of hate, jealousy and lies, was no nearer conclusion than before.

"What news from London?" she asked. "That is why we are here, alone, and the door closed, is it not?"

A smile streaked across his face. "True, but I wished to demonstrate how much I care for you."

She stepped close, placed a hand to his chest, and on tiptoe pressed her lips to his in a tender light kiss. A fleeting kiss, nevertheless it was open declaration of her feelings toward him, and mark of approval for more of the same when time might allow. No words were needed, eyes-locked they understood each other; fully.

She stepped back, he continued. "I received a letter from London, a day past. It was from Jack Pagent's wife, sadly, now his widow. Why me I pondered upon reading the first few lines, and then her words told of a drink sodden and broken man. A man she claimed she no longer knew. This being the man she had married that same year of the summer ball. In the last few months, apparently, nightmares had plagued him and so bad were they, he took his own life but a week back. His last words before walking out of the house, 'May Adam, Lord Brockenbury, rot in hell'."

"I see, and you think Adam's elevated lordly rank tipped Lieutenant Jack Pagent over the edge?"

"According to his wife Jack read an account of father's mysterious murder in the London Gazette the day prior. He then told her he knew who'd killed old Lord Brockenbury and why. He said it was to do with Adam's gambling debts and the Datchett girl. By that he meant Eliza, and I know where that leads us to."

"But we have—or rather you have it in mind Eliza did the terrible deed, is that not so?"

"I did. Now I am not so sure."

"Oh, so you think her innocent? Are you of mind Adam is looking to pin blame to Eliza just as he pinned James' suicide to me? For we both know he was murdered."

"There my love, now you see how easy it is to be set on the wrong path when seeking motive for murder."

Love, he'd referred to her as his love. She must not let it go to her head but such caused her heart to jolt and she glanced up at him.

He laughed, said, "I must be more careful when in the company of others." He caught up her hand, her wrist turned sufficient for him to place a kiss on her racing pulse. "Sorry. It just tripped off my tongue."

"Edwin, are you sure, really sure this is right for you? I fear regret may be yours sooner than you might wish. Scandal lingers like a foul mist, the ladies of the *ton* with kerchiefs to noses until such time as they decide stench of scandal has drifted away and of no consequence. True enough I saw not a kerchief to nose today, despite passing Lady Bathurst and the Honourable Charlotte Cavendish, nor did I spy such with lesser notables en route. And Rantchester could not have been more polite, bar placing his coat at my feet as Raleigh did for good Queen Bess."

"Rantchester, an elite of the *haut beau monde* stopped to pass the time of day with you, and here you are worrying your pretty head about foul mists of scandal. Oh Georgette, my beautiful, adorable Georgette. Why must you fret so?"

A manly sigh escaped, his expression almost that of amusement and markedly infuriating. "Most young ladies would be dancing with joy, bleating about heart flutters, hoping against hope a note declaring the marquis' interest would soon be winging its way to their hands."

"Heaven forbid that should happen."

Why? Would not such set your mind at rest in knowledge you can step out again in good heart."

69

"You mean no longer subjected to the indignity of ladies fluttering fans to shun the sinner in their midst, nor the snide comments heard from behind manly kerchiefs."

"Did you suffer those indignities?"

"On the night of the ball, yes, I did. Afterwards no, for I kept myself to myself."

"And now, would you been seen walking out with me?"

"Yes, but that cannot happen for the time being."

"Why not?"

"Because, because it is best that we are not seen together."

"I fear I have missed a clue along the way. Has something happened?"

"It has, and if Adam suspects for one moment you and I have feelings for one another, things could become very difficult."

"Then enlighten me, for I am standing here blind to events I know nothing of." He gestured to a chaise. She sat down, drew breath, and he sat next to her, her hand cupped in his. "Now, tell me what has happened."

Seven

What could be the matter? With a letter to hand, she said, "Why, why would Grandfather insist on coming here, to see me? It is a most urgent matter, his words so stern in countenance almost to that of treating me as though a wilful child." She cast the letter to lap, exasperation about her. "What matter could he possibly wish to discuss that could not have waited a few more days upon my return to London?"

Rose glanced up and likewise let fall her hands to lap, her deft fingers quick to thread her embroidery needle to linen and place it to one side. "Does he give no reason, no reason at all?"

"None, except to say he has business in Bath, that he arrived yesterday, and will call here at precisely four of afternoon."

Rose cast her eyes to the mantel clock. "Oh. Well. I had best make myself scarce."

"No, why should you? This is your house."

"Father's actually, and it seems he and your grandfather will arrive at about the same time."

"It is so unlike grandfather to throw dictate at me in this unreasonable manner."

"Then he must have good cause. Bear with him, Georgette, for he may have heard word of the troubles at Monkton Abbeyfields. It would not surprise me if he fears you are becoming embroiled in another scandal. You are after all, here, in Batheaston, not safe away in London."

"But he cannot think I had anything to do with Lord Brockenbury's murder."

71

Rose eased herself from her chair. "I think a lie down might do me well. That dreadful pain in my back is worse than before."

"Is it? Do you think— What I mean is. Could it be your soldier boy is wont to make himself known to us?"

"Praise be to God if that is so."

Georgette hastened to her feet. "Here, take my arm."

At that very moment the pull-bell clanged in the hall and Beatrice fair flew into the room, and in a mad rush of words said, "You are never going to believe who that is."

"Oh no," exclaimed Georgette, "not Adam Brockenbury?"

"Heavens no. It's the Marquis of Rantchester."

They all looked one to the other, and Rose winced indicating severe pain. It was not her back giving grievance it was most definitely her hoped for soldier boy. She clutched at her extended bump. "Get me upstairs and send word for Doctor Swanley."

"Take her arm," said Georgette, handing Rose to the care of Beatrice. "I shall send for Swanley right away."

As Beatrice assisted in getting Rose aloft, Georgette rushed after the footmen who had at that very instant opened the front door. She snatched at a silk shawl in passing and before the marquis could utter a word she grabbed his arm, whirled him about and plied him toward his waiting carriage. "Hurry— I need to get word to Doctor Swanley. Rose is having the baby."

"Struth", his first word, and then, "hop aboard, dear lady, and which way for my coachman?"

"Straight ahead and stop just after the bridge, at the house standing proud."

The driver needed no further instruction and as soon as both were seated, the carriage door closed and the Marquis of Rantchester's tiger clambered back onboard. The carriage lurched a little and the horses were soon whipped up and set to extended trot.

"What will you wager, boy or girl?" charged he, raking fingers through his wind riffled blond hair.

Astounded by the challenge, she said, "Wager? Wager on a baby? I think not."

The marquis grinned, leaned across the divide and in a hushed tone, said, "Davenport will be delighted with a boy, no doubt. I on the other hand would prefer a bevy of daughters before a son and heir pops a Peter out for all to see."

She blushed, for his inference suddenly dawned, and equal in whisper she said, "Must men always think that way, and by it, I presume you mean a son would be future competition in pursuit of flirty ladies of the *ton*?"

"You think me that much of a rogue, that I would marry and then seek brief affairs?" His dark brown eyes settled on hers. "No, for thoughts of sullying young virgins has never entered this head of mine. Damn it all, Georgette, a bold mistress ain't to be found amidst the svelte fillies of the *ton*, don't you know. Good grief, even the Regent likes 'em buxom, wedded and well knowing in how to please a man."

She blushed under his intense scrutiny. "Then I apologise most humble, for it is not something a lady is wont to concern herself with, anymore than whether a young gentleman is seeking a mistress from among the married ladies or that of untarnished miss. But now that I am aware that is so, I shall in future pay regard to gentlemen of the *beau monde* with great interest."

"I suppose your experience with Brockenbury did more harm than good, and reason enough for your taking flight at his ruffling your skirts. But why stay away from all the parties and balls for so long?"

73

"I never received invitations." She held her breath, the bridge upcoming, her heart in mouth as the carriage passed over the Avon faster than any coach she had travelled in before. "Not that I wanted to see Brockenbury again."

"Understandable, your ladyship, but there were other gentlemen, and plenty of 'em seeking you here, and seeking you there. Must confess I spied you out and about in a carriage early of evening one day whilst exercising my mount in Hyde Park. Never thought to make approach, for I assumed a lovers tryst was in the offing."

She had not noticed before but now, on eye-to-eye contact, she thought him a little pale around the jaw line. His once moderately handsome features were now hollow and drawn. She glanced beyond him, to the road ahead. "This is it," she said, in haste, the doctor's house a few yards hence, the horses already slowing on pace.

"Righty ho." As the carriage drew to a standstill he shouted back over his shoulder. "Jem, go knock for the doctor and tell him he's needed at Fenemore. A baby on the way."

"I might as well not have come if I am not to call on his services myself."

"You're a lady, Georgette Beaumont, not a maidservant to Mrs. Davenport."

"She's my friend, Beatrice too."

"Admirable girls both, for they stood by you when others shunned you."

"Exactly, I owe them."

He leaned forward again, hand to knee. "God knows I wish I had done more to protect you that night, and that's why I came to call upon you."

"To apologise for manhandling me? To beg forgiveness for having walked away when you knew exactly what Adam had in mind?"

74

"I held you back to spare you the sight of Adam fisting his brother. It was bound to happen. I knew that much. But James and what happened came as a complete shock. Believe it, Jack Pagent and I were as scared as you were. And then, to see you in Bath this week looking so pretty and vulnerable yet braving it out, an open carriage at that, my heart went out to you."

"Heart, you have a heart?"

He sat back as though a dagger thrust to heart, and for the second time she focused full attention to his face: a ghost of a man before her. He was nothing like she had seen only days ago in Bath.

"What have you done to yourself?"

"Done? Why nothing, beyond that of indulging in a pipe or two."

"Of exotic dream smoke?"

He chuckled. "Yes, a little of that too."

"It shows?"

"Did you smell it from number fourteen Brock Street, by any chance?"

"Oh, so that's why you were there, why Beatrice saw you loitering outside the end house."

"Yee Gods, Georgette, you really know how to make a man feel bad about himself." He raised his hand to prevent another word from her. "Happen you're right. Happen there is no hope for me. Happen I'm as dead as Lieutenant Jack Pagent, not in body, but in mind."

Jem returned. "The doctor'll be right along, soon as he's saddled his hoss, your lordship."

"Back to Fenemore, it is then."

Jem clambered aboard and the driver reined the horses to the right and brought them about as tight as able, but even then they failed to make a full turn. He reined them back a couple of strides and with verbal encouragement again

75

brought them about. This time they were facing back the way they had come and set off at a goodly trot, though the bridge once more caused Georgette to hold her breath.

As soon as clear of the bridge the marquis rose from his seat, stepped across the divide and sat down beside her. "This murder of old Brockenbury, any theories on who done it?"

"Was he murdered? I heard it was a hunting accident. Was it not a case of his out shooting and his somehow falling on a knife."

"You believe that story?"

"More to the point, why wouldn't I?"

"Have you not heard of Adam's proposed marriage to his cousin, the Datchett girl? A hefty dowry comes with the dark wench and more than enough to clear Adam's debts, but a first cousin for a wife?" He snorted. "A little risqué if you ask me and inadvisable. By all accounts, the chances are an heir might be odd looking indeed. That's why old Brockenbury wanted none of it, and said it would happen over his dead body. Well now, ain't that the truth."

"You mean Adam still intends to marry her?"

"Who else will have him debts and all? Who else has ten thousand pounds to her name?"

It was becoming clear to her now. No wonder Adam had declared undying love. He wanted *her* money, Beaumont money: her fifteen thousand pound dowry not to mention her allowance from her grandfather's estate, which amply trumped Eliza's dowry. And yet, she felt it could not be that simple, not if he and Eliza were already betrothed.

"Did you know he broached marriage to me? Tricked me into meeting up with him by pretending to be Edwin?"

"You and Edwin?" The marquis' face dropped. "I had no notion you and he—"

76

"We are not," she said, far too quickly, and although it was a fib it was a wise fib because she could not be sure if his paying visit was on Adam's behalf. "We have mutual interest, in particular, that of Ranulph's and Beatrice's future happiness."

"In that case, may I request your attendance at a little soiree I have planned a week from today? Not a grand affair, just a carriage picnic on Lansdowne Hill. A wager or two on the horses and a bit of innocent flirting all round."

Dare she? Yet if she did not, it might be construed she and Edwin were closer than she cared the marquis to presume as a given: or Adam for that matter.

"What say you, Georgette, will you come?"

"Yes, I will."

He smiled in appreciation then grimaced. "Dash it all. Back at Fenemore all too soon," he said, his eyes not leaving hers for a second, "and now I must let you escape my clutches."

Upon Jem's speedy way of leaping from a moving carriage and then the door open as soon as the horses were at a standstill, she had not expected Rantchester to alight, but he did and hand extended assisted in her stepping down.

"Until we meet again," his comment, a bow, and kiss to her hand before letting her escape him completely. "I shall call for you at thirty after ten of morn. Wouldn't want to miss the early races, now would we? Believe me when I say, I am sincere in this, Georgette. It is time to repent my former sins."

"I'll be here, waiting," her reply, as she stepped away from the carriage.

With quicksilver movement he took one stride forward, pulled the bell-rope, and then back to his carriage. She turned, he waved, she waved back, and the carriage drove off. The door opened, she stepped inside and for the first time in a long while she felt as though she had returned from a very long and lonely journey.

A warm glow embraced her, for the Marquis of Rantchester, one of the elite in the *beau monde*, had purposefully come to call on her, and if correct in her thinking, Adam Brockenbury was ignorant of Rantchester's visit and of his kind invitation.

A sigh escaped, and sense of renewed awakening gripped her. Nevertheless a little trepidation too fell about her, for she would encounter at close quarter those who had shunned her and spread malicious gossip about her: far and wide.

Lordy, how would Edwin take such news? Why had she not thought how it might appear to him? Thoughtless, thoughtless, selfish Georgette is exactly what he would think. After all, if news ever reached her of Edwin spied escorting a lady she would be devastated.

She must write to him. Explain. *But what could one say to justify acceptance of invitation to dine out with another man? What had she done? How was she to resolve this dilemma?*

A deep chuckle drifting from the drawing room stole her attention.

Oh well, there was nowhere to hide she had to face her grandfather along with Mr. Knightley, even though she would rather go to Rose.

In passing across the hallway, she turned to the maid who'd rushed to answer the door. "Be so kind as tell Miss Beatrice the doctor is on his way."

"Yes, your ladyship." With that the maid fled to the upper floor.

Georgette paused, but momentary, merely to regain sense of absolute composure. She then strode forth to the drawing room with flourish and a smile upon face. One thing she could always be sure of, her grandfather loved her with all his heart and she likewise adoring of him.

Eight

The roar of the crowd strafed the hillside, and supportive cries amidst horse owners seemed to ripple alone the line of carriages that had been almost nose to tail for two hours; the weather glorious and perfect for a day's racing. A couple of minor races had preceded the major race of the day, but men were now shouting for individual runners within the Bristol Cup, a race notorious as one of high stakes.

Rivalry between landowners and of those who owned vast tracts of Bristol and Bath and surrounding districts were truly a sight to behold. She could not help but smile, for the Duke of Beaufort was supportive of Bristol and Rantchester supportive of Bath, and it was no wonder the occasional glower passed one to the other.

Standing on the carriage seat to gain better view of the horses now coming over a rise in the down, the marquis overtly animated caused his carriage to rock quite violently upon slapping his thigh and verbally urging his race horse onward. Other gentlemen were equal in much the same fashion, and a few ladies round and about were little better upon sighting the first few horses galloping for the winners post. One or two waved their bonnets. Sometimes the strictest codes of etiquette within the *ton* were let slip at events such as this, and little scorn shown even from the matriarchs. The grand old ladies, unlike the younger fraternity, had laid discreet wagers on horses, while the men folk were bold in declaring allegiances and the laying of bets on the final outcome.

"*Flybynight*," yelled Rantchester, struggling to keep his balance, "fly my beauty, fly home to daddy."

Georgette laughed even more at his reference to daddy, for *Flybynight* did seem to pick up her heels and fly as though having heard his voice. "Can she do it, do you think?"

He shot a quick glance in her direction and grinned, and she could see devilment etched in his eyes. "She will. She's a Rantchester filly."

Flybynight did win, and Rantchester whooped and threw his hat in the air. He looked to the Duke of Beaufort nearby and shouted, "Told you she's unbeatable." He then leapt from the seat and drew her so quickly into his embrace she had no chance to avoid it, any more than the kiss, albeit a momentary kiss. His exuberance was such that he'd barely realised what he had done. And she only too glad the ladies of the *ton* were too preoccupied with assessing their winnings. Nonetheless, she would have preferred it if Adam had been absent and not there with Eliza, which he was and no more than four carriages distant. *What if he should let slip to Edwin, of the marquis' momentary close encounter?*

"Sorry about that," said Rantchester, a big grin, and without further preamble he leapt from the carriage and strode off toward the Duke. She watched them shake hands in convivial manner and then heads together the pair stalked off to greet respective mounts and jockeys. The Duke was now forced to hand over the cup; reluctantly, but proffered it forth in jovial manner.

She glanced about her, and at a short distance in the carriage directly behind was none other than Lady Georgina Bathurst, whom waved and said, "Good morning's racing, Georgette, what say you?"

It gladdened her heart to think Countess Bathurst had kept her approach informal, for there was now no need to stand on ceremony. The lady, although senior in years with four sons and two daughters, good times had been shared between her parents and the Bathurst's in the past, and perhaps, not so easily forgotten after all. "Fine racing," she said, quite aware the senior lady had a speculative expression, "and how lucky we are with the weather."

"You must both come over to us for dinner one evening," by which, Georgette presumed to mean her and the marquis. "I understand you are staying with the Knightleys."

"For a few days more, and then back to London."

"Oh, what a pity." Her ladyship ordered her driver to lead on and draw alongside, which he did, and comfortably face to face, she further said: "What say you to dinner tonight, then?"

"We'd be delighted," said Rantchester, now returned with the Bristol Cup in his hand, "would we not, Georgette?"

"Well, I—"

"Grand," said the countess, hand slapped to knee. "Dinner at nine it is, and now, before I set off, what did the Knightley girl get from God's nursery?"

"A boy, a beautiful boy possessed of long black eye-lashes and shock of black hair."

"I'll lay twenty guineas the fluff will be gone within the fortnight and the boy will be as blond as Adonis within the year. Just like his father." Countess Bathurst then turned to Rantchester. "Did you rob Beaufort blind?"

"I did, and he wants *Flybynight* at any price."

"You'll not sell?"

"Never."

"Until later, then, Georgette." Her ladyship smiled. "We have much to catch up on, you and I, but I am now wont to retreat to the cool of my town house. The noon day sun," she muttered, face fanned most vigorous, "is utterly beyond comfort."

As they watched her ladyship's carriage driven away, Rantchester, said, "Would you prefer I have the carriage pulled out of line and a quiet spot found for our picnic? I have no other horses racing today and no inclination to favour any of Beaufort's in upcoming races." He bowed; a big smile. "I am now yours to command."

"Then let us retreat, for Lord Brockenbury is almost within hearing distance."

"Oh wicked lady, we shall away to a leafy bough I know quite well." He cast a glance along the line of carriages to their rear. "It seems he, too, has it in mind to leave and is coming this way."

She must not turn round. Must not give Adam the chance to make eye contact, and thankfully the marquis chose to sit opposite with his back to the team of fine chestnut geldings and therefore face on to Adam. And to his driver, Rantchester said, "Onward to the Oak, but give sway to Brockenbury's new curricle."

As the team began to pull out of line, she kept her eyes to the racetrack and the many carriages still surrounding the upper half of the track. One or two ladies glanced their way and acknowledged with fans waved in friendly gesture and polite smiles in mutual exchange. Their men folk cheered the marquis and extended congratulations on his fine win of the day. However, it was not long before Adam caused the marquis' team to falter, for his curricle drew level in the manner more that of a war chariot.

She flinched at every strike of his whip to horseflesh. It was so merciless and unnecessary. Thankfully Rantchester was quick to speak in defence of the horse, "Give it more head, dear fellow, and less of the whip and yon filly will give years of service in traces and make for a fine brood mare."

Adam's response was not the least unexpected. "Barely broken in, and a firm hand needed yet awhile, 'til she finally yields to my pleasure."

Rantchester parried in return. "Soft hands will result in a good mouth and a thoroughly pleasurable ride and drive thence onward."

Adam lashed his whip at his grey filly, its white of eye indicative of fear and its head reared high ever resistant to heavy hands on the rein. Georgette empathised with the animal, its mouth already frothed and it was slavered about the loins: a reminder of Adam atop her in the hayloft and equally unbearable.

His response to the marquis' outburst was, as always, purposeful in manner, "Be warned. The filly you now favour has a wild streak, too, and every bit as wilful as this grey."

Rantchester rallied to his feet in gallant manner rage stamped on his face, but Adam's grey took flight at a vicious twitch to her hindquarter. "Damn the man's insults. If ever a man needed a lesson in how to treat a woman it's Adam Brockenbury." He sat down again. "By jove that dark miss sitting alongside looks the part, if not of actual courage enough to set about him with a carriage whip."

"Perhaps she will."

He laughed. "Do you know the wench?"

"I had hoped you might be able to enlighten me, for I know little of her or how she came to be at Monkton Abbeyfields. On balance, since that awful night of the summer ball I have been somewhat lacking in knowledge all things the Brockenbury family. The Knightley girls are no better informed, for Ranulph barely mentions his family. And who can blame Beatrice for being wary of invites to houses where Adam might be in attendance, more especially after her encounter with him that night of the summer ball?"

He looked at her, curiosity in eye and wise countenance about him. "I have it in mind you don't altogether trust my motive for this day out. Less so after that farcical performance put on by Brockenbury. Well, let me reassure you, Georgette;

he and I had a parting of the ways some time ago."

"May I ask why, or is it a man thing?"

"In some ways, yes, a man thing. However, when opportunity of a moment alone and no one is within hearing distance, there is something I wish to discuss with you."

"Is it to do with the night of the summer ball?"

"That and something else."

As they drove onward she noticed Adam had reined in alongside Countess Bathurst's carriage and driving abreast of it. It seemed as though Eliza and the lady were well acquainted. "Do you suppose Adam and Eliza will be in attendance this evening at Lady B's dinner party?"

"Waylaid her, has he?" asked Rantchester, far too much of a gentleman to glance over his shoulder.

"If anything, I think it was Miss Datchett who waylaid her ladyship, and they do appear quite intimate in manner."

"Damn the man. Can we never escape him?" His outburst sounded heartfelt, and perhaps, like her, Rantchester truly wished to distance himself from Adam Brockenbury. "Too late now to back out," furthered he; emitting a sigh. "We're committed."

"At least we shall have each other for company, though I confess after dinner niceties may well prove a little unnerving."

"Georgette, my dearest lady, you were once the toast of the *beau monde*, and your mother a patroness of Almack's. Such is not forgotten, and why you sought to hide yourself away is beyond the comprehension of many of us. Damn it all, The Regent cavorts with his mistress in public. And scandals are rare in falling ruinous on aristocrats' heads, unless debt-ridden and declared insolvent. Hypocrisy at its worst, I grant you. Nonetheless supremely advantageous to the likes of us, for if you were simply of the gentry as are the Kightley clan, your chances of a step back up the social ladder would be nigh impossible after that caper in the hayloft."

"Caper?"

"Apologies angel, that was hard-hearted and inconsiderate of me. My behaviour that night was unforgivable."

Discussing private matters and inner fears whilst a driver was seated up front and tiger behind, was not exactly of her choosing. She cast her gaze from the marquis' face and he graciously accepted their conversation was terminated: until the carriage came to a standstill beneath a magnificent oak tree at the edge of a small copse.

"I am utterly famished," said he, alighting from the carriage before Jem had even turned, let alone leapt down to carry out his routine tasks. "Stay where are you, Jem" the marquis' commanded, whilst duly hauling a picnic hamper from the carriage along with a carriage rug. "Right, be off with the pair of you, and back here within two hours," his instructions to the driver.

The carriage rolled away and left to their own devices Rantchester spread out the rug and said, "This is where we go native and perch our arses on the ground." She laughed, she couldn't help herself, for he discarded his hat and jacket and further said, "The Lady first."

She settled to the rug rather glad of the cool shade afforded by the tree's overhead canopy. "It's a lovely spot up here, and a glorious view over Bristol."

"It is," his reply, the picnic hamper to hand. "Now, what have we got to munch on?"

She glanced to her left, Bath below them, then back at Rantchester. "How did you find this heavenly place?"

He grinned, game pie already to mouth; a bite taken. "An assignation with a lady of note years ago." He chewed on his pie, then said, "Memorable day, for I lost my virginity." He swallowed, and laughed heartily. "I see you're not shocked, which brings me to why I asked you out today." He gestured to the hamper. "Eat, please, or I shall feel less than a gentleman whilst sat here stuffing my face."

She surveyed the basket, as he in turn leaned forward and drew forth a small silver engraved flagon and two silver goblets.

"Goodness, who prepared all this for you?"

He chuckled. "My cook and I won't do without her. She goes where I go and sees me proud for whatever I demand of her."

"Well, cook most certainly sees right by you." She selected a stuffed apricot, a mere bite delicious. "Oh my goodness, what does this filling consist of?"

"Chopped hazelnuts, herbs, ginger, lamb and apricot." He glanced at her then, a goblet extended and half filled with claret coloured liquid. "Why do women have to know what it is they are eating?" He shook his head, clearly amused at her reticence to accept the wine. "Drink up, it's not poisoned." Again he looked her in the eye. "About that night of the summer ball."

Her trust in him now assured, she accepted the goblet and fibbed outright. "I must tell you; some aspects of that night still elude me. I simply cannot remember."

He drained his goblet in one swig, his eyes settling on hers. "I wish; for I remember it all too well." He refilled his goblet, glanced skyward. "Damn it all, dragging up the past on a day like this, I must be mad."

"But necessary; is it not?"

"Think me a fool if you must, but since Jack Pagent's suicide I've thought long and hard about James' suicide." He faltered, poured more wine and gulped it back in one. "Damn it to hell, why don't I just spill forth what has caused sleepless nights of late."

"It might help in setting your mind to rest, for whatever is troubling you, has taken its toll, as I can see."

"I could be wrong but I think Adam murdered James."

She hoped she looked sufficiently shocked at his statement. "But why? Why would Adam kill his own brother?"

He again let fall his eyes to hers. "You remember how it was that night, and James so drunk he had not a clue what he had said to you. Nor I think, did he understand how he had ended up in the stable yard. Poor fellow had looked and sounded utterly confused when we three came up behind you both."

"That's when you and Jack grabbed hold of me and hauled me into the coach house."

"Believe me, Georgette, when I say; we had no knowledge of a pistol in Adam's possession that night. When in London, yes, we armed ourselves for walking out and about, and where Adam favoured a pistol, Jack and I had daggers secreted in our boots."

"But did it not cross your minds what Adam's intentions

were? You knew him. You were his friends. You knew what he was about with Beatrice Knightley, and yet you stood back and watched from the shadows."

"We were drunk, too, and not really thinking all that straight at the time. What he did with the young Knightley girl we looked upon it as just a bit of tomfoolery."

"For you, but not for Beatrice. She thought him in love with her. Naïve to be sure, but at barely fifteen she was easily influenced by his attentions upon her. And then what he did to me, and how he lied afterwards. You stood there in front of the assembled and let Adam tell all how James had discovered us in the hayloft, and then how James had stormed off and shot himself."

"I dare say my sins will catch up with me, yet." He refilled his goblet and swigged the contents in one gulp. "Jack's death. I don't believe it was suicide."

She sat quiet, aware Rantchester found solace in wine. What could she say?

"Georgette, speak to me. Tell me what you're thinking."

She too sipped at her wine, her thoughts galloping this way and that. She drew breath, heart palpitating and sense of fear gripping her. "Do you feel at all threatened by Adam, as I do? I can't explain what it is that I feel for sure, but dread grips me whenever he's nearby. And yet when we first met, I confess I was mildly attracted to him."

He reached across and gently laid his hand upon hers. "I am resigned to my fate. No doubt an unpleasant encounter with strangers down a dark alley one night will be my lot. But I will fight and endeavour to survive rather than perish."

"Are you suggesting Adam wants you dead?"

"The last witness to events leading up to James' death, of course he wants me dead."

"But I was there, too."

"You saw nothing of the shooting, nor did I. You're quite safe because Adam is obsessed with you. However, Jack said he saw what happened and threatened Adam he was going to go to the newspapers unless Adam paid him to keep his mouth shut. Jack might have witnessed the wicked deed. I cannot be sure about that, for you and I were grappling with each other. However, is it not credible for Adam to suppose Jack revealed all to me?"

"And Lord Brockenbury's death?"

"Cause for concern."

"Indeed."

"Georgette, I am a fool in many ways, but Edwin Brockenbury is not, and I have it on good authority his father's death will not go unpunished. He and the Constable are reinvestigating the night of the summer ball, albeit with the utmost discretion. To which I have offered assistance in any way I can."

"But if Adam finds out—"

"I trust Edwin Brockenbury. No more to be said, except I want to see you happy once again and dancing and flirting with admirers swarming about you. I cannot imagine the heartache you must have suffered, though I do know something of loneliness."

"The Marquis of Rantchester; lonely?"

"One can be lonely in company, and no one else the wiser."

"I know something of that, too."

"Then we are a sorry pair, but again friends, I trust."

"Friends."

"Will you marry Edwin if he asks?"

"What made you ask that, of all things?"

"A secret source. And if true, feel free to regard me as your partner in any masquerade you think necessary. It would be extreme wise to let Adam think my affections for you are reciprocated, which indeed sets Edwin free from overt scrutiny and affords more chance of his delving where others have no access."

"Has he asked this of you?"

"Not as such but it does seem my fate is that of procuring happiness for others whilst such continues to elude me."

"Then perhaps I can assist in procuring a happy outcome for you, though not an easy task; I might add. Your dance steps are shameful in presentation, and I in the past oft given to sore toes after more than one dance with you."

He laughed. "A dance mistress, you propose yourself as my dance mistress? Be damned you're a brave woman to take on that task."

"It might help."

"Then so be it." He laughed again. "Well then Georgette, we have a new understanding between us." He scrambled to his feet. "A bush methinks. I need a stroll behind a bush." He winked and began striding toward a furze, its yellow haze of blossoms glorious. He then paused, turned and said, "If you need a stroll, I am the perfect knight and always keep my back turned."

"Thank you, no. But if I need to I will ask that you come and stand guard."

"So straight home with you, once our picnic is over?"

"I do recall your ordering the carriage to be returned within two hours, and perhaps by then afternoon tea; most fitting upon our return to Fenemore. Beatrice is a dab-hand at toasting muffins."

"Done," said he in response, afore disappearing from sight.

A few moments later a loud hiss from his lordship attracted her attention. "You have to see this, or you'll never believe it."

Nine

Georgette held her tongue.

"Were they?" squealed Beatrice. "Oh lordy, and you saw them?"

The marquis laughed. "Ah, but you see, I know how much you ladies love titillating gossip, and forgive me, for I was not alone in my observations."

Beatrice's eyes swung to Georgette, "You too?"

"Well, yes, but I did avert my eyes almost immediately."

"But you witnessed the pair, nonetheless."

"Yes, and I wish I had not, for it was—" She dare not reveal the full extent of what had occurred, the manner of its execution beastlike, though apparently not so unusual for a member of the notorious *Hell Fire Club*. Quite sure Rantchester would be less charitable in relaying turn of events within the confines of *Watie'rs Club*, she re-gathered her flow, "It was Adam Brockenbury at his worst in a manner unbecoming a gentleman of note."

"Wait 'til I tell Ranulph."

"Do you think you should?" intoned Rose, her eyes revealing great knowledge all things men and sexual appetites. "Mere titillating gossip for us can be— well— somewhat stimulating for a gentleman."

"I am most gratified you kept your eyes averted whilst passing admirable advice to your sister," proffered Rantchester, a big grin.

Rose, quite bold, looked him in the eye and declared, "I dare say your feet idled in retreat, unlike Georgette's."

Having been Rantchester's guest at the races and a thoroughly wonderful afternoon in his company Georgette felt

95

it her duty to defend him, and said, "Oh Rose, it was an awkward moment all round, and we had no prior knowledge of their presence, and they thankfully remained unaware of ours."

Beatrice's eyes lit up. "And why were you two walking through the bushes?"

"Pray to heaven I am not about to be labelled a cad?"

Rose laughed at Rantchester's outburst. "I think I know Georgette well enough, and I suspect it was you who lit upon the lovers and then relayed your findings. Women are not oft given to walking through wild bushes unless in company with another woman, and unexpected circumstance prevails."

"True enough, dear lady, and my need for bush walking was circumstance driven indeed." Rantchester, not the least fazed by Rose' astute scrutiny, furthered with, "But then, you are a married woman and know of these things."

"Quite," remarked Rose, a hint of a smile.

Oh goodness, Rose had quite misunderstood Rantchester's need for a bush. *Or had she*? Georgette glanced at the marquis, and their eyes collided, and something within those laughing orbs suggested Rose was right and herself wrong. She sensed colour flooding her cheeks, for she had thought excessive intake of liquid had driven him to the bushes. But now, the truth was written on his face.

He smiled and alighted from his seat and addressed Beatrice, "You toast muffins to perfection, Miss Knightley. He then addressed Rose. "Mrs. Davenport, I thank you for your gracious invite to take tea with three of the most beautiful and charming creatures in the district. Alas, an evening engagement calls this man home to re-dress." It was then her turn for those wicked brown eyes settled on her. "Georgette, I shall see you later, and if it would suit you my carriage will call at around eight of the clock."

"That will suit me fine."

"Good. I shall await your arrival at my house and although it is but a short stroll to Georgia's residence, I shall ride with you." He clicked his heels together, his soldier past still ingrained. He bowed. "Until tonight."

Rose had already tugged on the servant's bell-rope. The door opened quite prompt and Rantchester left the room accompanied by Mr. Knightley's manservant. Silence then befell them until the marquis' carriage wheels were heard rumbling from the yard.

"Now that he's gone," enthused Beatrice, eyes agog and her hands cupping ears, "do tell us what you saw, what beastly Brockenbury and that witch of his were doing."

"*Witch?*" exclaimed Rose. "You must not say such things, B."

"Eliza looks the part, and Ranulph has her depicted as a witch in one of his paintings."

"Well, I don't know which of you two is wickeder. Shame on Ranulph."

Beatrice laughed. "Why must you always sound like a grand dame imposing chivalrous and demure behaviour upon young people?"

"Because I am the eldest and it is my place to set an example to you, the younger."

"Such makes you appear older than your years. And I pity Frederick on his return, for you have become quite staid since giving birth to Frederick junior." Beatrice's face then beamed with wicked glee. "And, by all accounts Frederick junior came earlier than expected, and yet, according to the doctor he was born full term. Are we to suppose, Georgette and I, that you and Frederick took walks

97

in the bushes quite often before you were wed?"

Rose blushed prettily and smiled and braved her sister's insinuation. "Passion is the very devil at times, that is why I worry for you and Ranulph and wish to see you both settled before your lives are blighted by little ones about the house."

Georgette stepped in. "I grant Rose understood Rantchester's reasons for a walk in the bushes long before I did, and it was most gentlemanly for him to retreat rather than display his ardour."

Beatrice looked at her in wonderment. "Oooh Georgette, you mean— Oh, my goodness. Did he?"

"I assume so, for I had not thought to look, and had not dreamed such had entered his mind."

"But he invited you to the races, and you both partook of a picnic, alone. Did it really not cross your mind he might have great regard for you, or at best interest sufficient to fire him with passion?"

Rose giggled. Her dame-hood of righteousness and propriety cast aside. "Set on fire by passion? It is base desire that causes a man to hide in the brush alone, and fatal if his lady is of like-mind."

Beatrice' smile broadened, and the sudden flush to her cheeks was unmistakable and indicative of guilt. "But we do tease, mercilessly, and it thrills us to think a man is so enamoured with our charms that a little interest is sometimes apparent below decks."

"B, you must be careful, very careful in your dealings with Ranulph. In spite of everything, he's no lesser a man than the others."

Georgette felt Rose was being a little unfair to Beatrice and Ranulph. "I'm sure she's most careful, Rose, and sensible with it."

"I do hope so, though I suspect she's a clever little minx and given to ways of distracting the maid sent along as chaperone."

The doorbell clanged, and with bated breath they listened in silence each wondering who it could be at the door at five of afternoon. No one was expected. A moment or two passed before the door was tapped and Mr. Knightley's manservant entered a letter on silver tray. "For her ladyship."

"Thank you," said Rose, which signalled for him to deliver said letter to its recipient.

Even as Georgette reached for it she sensed fate might be about to play a cruel trick upon her.

As the manservant turned about she broke open the seal.

Beatrice and Rose fell to hushed conversation whilst she browsed the letter's content.

"Oh no, not now," exclaimed Georgette. "Not when I'm away from him."

"Bad news?" asked Rose.

"The worst news possible. It's from Edwin. He says, *Dear Georgette, It is with sincere heartfelt sympathy that I write this letter to inform you of your grandfather's sudden ill health, and much regret for the haste and unseemly time in which it will reach your hands. Immediate return to your abode in London would be wise given his grace's yearning for your presence. His physician is of the opinion anyone who wishes to talk with him must do so within the next couple of days. I fear it unwise to reveal the circumstance leading up to this untimely event, and trust you will accommodate my intervention in this matter.* He's signed it, *lawyer and confidante to his Grace, Duke of Retford. Edwin Brockenbury*".

She sniffled, fighting back tears. "Since when did Edwin become grandfather's confidante, let alone his lawyer?

Though it matters not, for I must get back to London, and to accomplish that I need wheels." She looked to Rose. "Would it be possible to send young Tucker with a message to Rantchester?"

"But of course. It is his job to run messages and fetch and deliver. He can take the trap."

"With Grandfather grave ill, I cannot attend a dinner party with heavy heart."

"And you wish to return to London tomorrow first thing?"

"I do, but will I be able to secure a drag at such short notice?"

"That might pose a problem, and you cannot go by mail coach, it is far too rough for a lady of your standing."

"I dare say it's fully booked," said Beatrice, a tentative smile. "It always looks overloaded when it goes past the house, and as Rose said, not a nice way for a lady to travel."

"If needs must, and they do, even a hay wagon would suffice."

Rose waved her hands ushering her out of the room. "Go to the library and write a letter for the marquis. And Beatrice, get Tucker to make ready to leave." Orders given, Rose followed on their heels, "I must away to the nursery and my son."

Ten

How very kind of him.

She had not expected Rantchester to rally to her cause but he had, and despite several stops en route to rest the horses and partake of refreshments they had finally reached London by late eventide: the clock on the mantel having declared ten-minutes past six.

Eleven heart-rending hours of travelling, and it was now thirty minutes after eight and dinner due at nine, but she had little appetite to speak of.

Glancing around the opulent salon where her grandfather had always welcomed his guests, she was struck by the quietude of the house bar for the ticking clock on the mantel. The silk clad walls of peacock blue were all a shimmer beneath flickering candle glow from the overhead chandeliers. The mellowed oak panelling appeared as though specked with gold; a reminder of childhood and of fanciful imaginings. Oh how she wished, truly wished she could step back in time to recapture something taken from her, something that could never be regained.

She visualised her mother and father, who in like to grandfather, had always received friends in this very room. Never allowed in attendance, but sufficiently wilful in escaping her governess, she had so oft sat on the top stair watching the beautiful people below. A hasty retreat was often called for upon a footman slipping past her to inform her father that dinner would be served in five minutes.

Who could have thought a dreadful coaching accident in winter would steal her parents away, thus her happy childhood thence shattered into jagged pieces of memory.

Elements of that awful evening haunted her, and worse, on her and grandfather's return from his country estate where her parents had perished, this very house although empty was bearable because he was with her. Similar air of quietness now prevailed. It was the hushed silence of a house in mourning. How she missed them, all of them, and now here she was truly alone, and a new Duke of Retford would soon take possession of her grandfather's estate and this very house.

"Will you stay with the Knightleys' for awhile or settle to your new home?"

She glanced at Rantchester seated on a chaise near to a window, the ever-elegant marquis: handsome and good company. "The Knightley girls are my truest friends. And yet, at the same time I do not wish to impose upon their kindliness."

"There is always my house in the *Crescent*, and you are most welcome to stay." A tentative smile creased his face. "If you wish, for sake of propriety, I can vacate the Bath town house and return to my father's country abode. London at this time of the year is too damn putrid."

"I think, perhaps, I shall set about my new house straight away. To stay at your fine city abode, even if you remained absent it might be construed I am your mistress. So mine it is, and I shall see what needs to be done, or not, for if I keep busy I shall have no time to dwell on today's sad event. My greatest regret will forever be that I failed to get here in time, failed to be here at his leaving. I think he must have known he was ailing, yet he had prior said nothing of his illness."

"He's with you in spirit, Georgette, and yon portrait over the mantel will no doubt comfort you when need arises."

She glanced up at her grandfather's portrait: a man of supreme elegance and exceedingly handsomeness in

features. Although depicted with white hair, white moustache, he nonetheless had a wicked sparkle in his green eyes. Despite
advanced years his back had remained as straight as an arrow shaft, and lean in stature he was a man to be seriously reckoned with in any fencing match. *Who would have suspected a weakened heart*?

"Do you suppose I can remove the portrait? After all, the house from this day forward belongs to a distant relative, whom I've never met, nor can I remember grandfather ever having made mention of his name."

"If the new duke has never paid visit then a replacement portrait will suffice. There must be others in the house of the same size or larger."

"Oh wicked man. You think I dare swap it?"

"Why not? Who is to know? But are the portraits the property of the new owner? What exactly is entailed within the titled deeds?"

"I imagine everything will be his. The only thing I can be sure about is the house and land in Somerset, which grandfather purchased for me. It's rather sad, for he was in Bath and I had no knowledge of his presence there until he sent word to say he would be calling at Fenemore. I naturally thought the worst. I felt sure he must have read of the late Lord Brockenbury's death, and I had quite expected him to demand my return to London with immediate effect to avoid my name becoming linked to the tragedy. But no, he had made the journey in order to secure my future, just in case marriage eluded me due to the scandalous tag already about my neck."

Rantchester chuckled, his attention half in the room half in the street beyond the window. "That particular scandal was all hot air on the night and as good as forgotten within a couple of months. You could have stepped out with the devil himself a month later, and not a soul would have raised an eyebrow." He suddenly sat up straight and peered in earnest through the window. "Well I'll be damned."

"What do you see?"

"The Regent, and by jingo, he has a new mistress, methinks"

She rushed to the window, a hand laid to Rantchester's shoulder for support whilst leaning forward to better gain view of the royal personage and his lady, or not so ladylike companion; both now passing along the street.

"Oh my goodness, that's a very dramatic red and black gown and extremely theatrical feathers atop her bonnet."

"Bonnet? Is it not a turkey on the woman's head?"

She laughed in spite of the reason for their being there, but Rantchester seized the moment by placing a kiss to her hand.

"Georgette, my lovely, all the turkey feathers in the kingdom cannot turn a tart into a lady. And yet, a lady could do well to learn the bedchamber manners of a tart and perchance, keep a husband true."

In haste she withdrew her hand from his shoulder and stepped back. "Then why do so many wives seek a lover?"

"Touché," said he, a broad grin. "Strike a man deep, why don't you."

"Am I a fool then to suppose mutual love and passion will be insufficient to keep you true to a wife? For I am supposedly your mistress of the dance and my precious time is to be given in attempt at bettering your chances of a love match."

"Marry me, Georgette, and never a truer man could you find."

"But I cannot marry you, and you know perfectly well why that is so."

"Are you absolutely sure a Brockenbury is right for you?"

"Adam as a future brother-in-law is enough to fill any potential Brockenbury wife with dread, and no, I am not absolutely sure about any blessed thing at present."

"Then marry me and be done with the Brockenburys."

"I shall ask you to leave if you persist in this matter of pressing for marital engagement."

"Tease, dear lady, mere tease. And it has, I think, lightened your heart a little."

He was right, more serious matters had for the moment passed her by and for that she was sincerely grateful. But his repartee declared as mere tease was suspect indeed.

She glanced at the mantel clock: dinner in five minutes. *Where was Edwin*? He had promised to be back within the hour.

She sensed tears welling and fought to restrain them, but one escaped and trickled down her cheek, and then another, and as much as she despised her weakness she gave sway to the inevitable.

Rantchester leapt to his feet not a word spoken, handkerchief given, his shoulder offered, accepted and his embrace if nothing else afforded sense of safeness and comfort.

"I am so sorry, so sorry," said she, grateful for his company. "I tried my best, but it's difficult, so very difficult to think of him as gone, and—"

"Shush, it's all right, angel."

Just as her grandfather had fifteen years beforehand, Rantchester kissed her head and tightened his embrace. Suddenly a memory, a hazy memory of an upturned carriage in a snowy landscape leapt to the forefront of her mind.

"I was there. I was there. It's all coming back to me. Oh God. How could I forget such a thing?"

Rantchester eased her away from his chest, "Forget? Forget what?"

"We were travelling to the country, to grandfather's estate. It was very cold as I remember, a bitter wind blowing and it began to snow. Mother wanted to stop at a coaching inn at Banbury, as I recall, but father ordered the coach onward in the belief we could reach the estate before the roads became impassable. Then a blizzard came down upon us, and although the horses kept to a steady trot I doubted they were able to see the way ahead any more than our driver could. Father stubborn and proud said *'horses could sense their way home'*. We did reach the estate, and when safely through the gates the coach had to descend a steep incline and that is when it happened. The coach slewed sideways, tipped over and slid down the side of the hill dragging the horses with it, and—"

"And?"

"And— and— I must have bumped my head, but I do remember the cold, feeling oh so very cold, and grandfather's voice. Yet I was safe in the house and grandfather hugging me tight in his arms. How is it possible to remember it now, when I had always thought of the accident as something that happened to my parents, not I?"

"How old were you?"

"Seven. It was my birthday and that is why we were going to the country.

"Strange things can happen to the mind, as I know to my cost when I fell from a horse at the gallop. I had no recollection of the accident or why it had occurred, yet all the bruises and aches and pains were evidence of the fall itself, and I of course on my arse and no horse. Several weeks later whilst out riding with friends we encountered a viper snoozing on open heath land, and I then remembered the events leading up to my accidental tumble. A viper startled by my horse struck out whilst riding past the damnable reptile, which caused my horse to lunge sideways. In turn my foot slipped from the stirrup and upon the horse bolting and dodging a fence rather than jump it, I hit the ground with a resounding wallop."

"Ouch." She dabbed at tears, and aware the front door had opened and closed shut again, said, "That must be Edwin."

It was her beloved, and he soon entered the room a swathe of legal documents in hand, his expression wary as though things were not quite as expected. "All very unprofessional," he said, placing the ribbon-bound documents on a chair, "to allow interested parties a glimpse of the will before the reading." He unbuttoned his jacket, his grey eyes coming to rest on hers and she sensed air of coldness about him, more so when he said, "Will you return to Bath soon after the funeral?"

"I presume the duke will want immediate possession of this house, so yes, I shall return to Bath. There is nothing here for me now; and London in summer, I think not."

As soon as said she wished the words unsaid, for something in his eyes declared he thought Rantchester's swift retreat from her side as that of guilt and prior intimacy between them. She could not let such thoughts fester, for her heart was Edwin's and no other's.

"Edwin, when I said nothing here for me, it was not meant as said, for I shall need your guidance in the coming days. However, it would be unwise to stay here after Friday. It would be wrong to expect the new duke to take pity on me so that I can remain in London at my leisure."

Edwin's face remained expressionless, his tone quite

formal. "As it is I too shall return to Abbeyfields as soon as the late duke's business is finally concluded, and thence to further my aims in bringing justice to bear on my father's killer. Thank the Lord the Constable's men came upon a drover passing through on his way to London a few days ago. The man recalled having spied a horseman in the field near to the bridge on the day the murder occurred. The rider was so fierce in argument with a man on foot, the drover slipped past unnoticed and hurried on his way."

She sensed Edwin ill at ease and setting precedence for detachment as though there was nothing between them anymore. What had happened to cause this coldness about him? She wished Rantchester gone from the room, and worse he stole the moment:

"Good news indeed and we are agreed on Jack's death as that of murder, are we not?"

"We are," said Edwin, "and in lieu of substantial reward put forth for information two men came forward, and *dei gratia* we may have Jack's killer in custody by the morrow."

"Right, I shall away to my club," said Rantchester, stepping away from the window, "my carriage has just arrived."

Edwin's expression was that of confusion. "You're leaving?"

"Georgette and I agreed a while back that I would retreat as soon as able, though I had seriously begun to think a penny in advance to a street urchin a damnable mistake. But no, the honourable little chap has quite obviously delivered a message to the coaching inn where my driver and team were laid up, and I shall now reward his honesty with a further tuppence." Rantchester bowed but momentary. "I shall return here as agreed on Thursday, and escort Georgette back to Bath on the afternoon of Friday."

It was terribly bold but she stepped forward and placed a kiss on Rantchester's cheek. "You've been a good friend to me, Rupert, and extreme gallant and very understanding of my needs in this matter of grandfather's— Well, you know what I mean, and I have so enjoyed your companionship."

"My pleasure, and take the portrait and be damned. It morally belongs with you."

Rantchester smiled, turned on his heels and Edwin saw him out and into the hall. And as always, discretion the watchword of the footmen, they relinquished their duties and left Rantchester and Edwin in private exchange.

Why though had Edwin looked accusatory, as though suspecting duplicity afoot?

Whilst awaiting his return she could not help but ponder over why so many young ladies had overlooked Rantchester's inner kindliness, for since his parting of the ways with Adam Brockenbury, the marquis had changed for the better.

She heard a loud and cheery farewell from Rantchester, and then momentary silence hung heavy before Edwin returned to the room, his handsome face blank as though a mask to hide inner feelings.

She feared he thought the worst of her, and when he said, "I know how it is between you and Rantchester," his tone so cold and cutting, her heart stalled.

"I feel accused, Edwin, of something I know nothing of."

"Your hand on his shoulder and a tender kiss."

"But how— Where were you?"

"Across the street. I paused to let the Regent drive past, and turned back a few strides before I could bear to walk through the door."

"It was an affectionate kiss, and meant nothing to me."

"It meant a lot to Rantchester. Believe it, I know the mere thrill derived from physical contact, and that kiss was open declaration of intent."

The less she said, the better, but she would not be accused of deceit. "It was wasted on me if that be the case, for I regard him as a good friend. That is all." She turned to her grandfather's portrait. "Do you think I can dare take him with me?"

"If I remember correctly, all portraits, paintings, crystal, silverware and copperware to be found in this house are bequeathed to you, along with furniture from your own private rooms and a substantive quantity of linen. The carriage and team of four it is suggested, only suggested, you may wish to retain or sell them on. There are property holdings in Bath and all secured in your name as surety of income derived from tenanted rental. This house, the remainder of its contents and your late grandfather's family seat in its entirety is entailed to the new duke."

"Who is?"

"A Lieutenant Rufus Meredith, who it seems is a young naval officer of heroic note, though of little monies to speak of."

She let fall her eyes from her grandfather's portrait and once again turned to Edwin. "Then I wish him well, and I shall hope this house will be loved by Rufus Duke of Retford as it was by my father and grandfather alike. And surely, a man of little monies will truly appreciate the estate and all it has to offer."

"And you, Georgette, what will you do, come Friday? Go with Rantchester and return to Fenemore, or to *your* house?"

She stepped toward him, for Rantchester's suggestive remark of a lady doing well to learn the ways of a mistress urged her to reach up and kiss Edwin on the lips, her reply: "I think that all depends on what you would have me do."

A smile flickered across his face, but momentary. "It is most difficult to put into words what I felt upon seeing Rantchester and yourself by the window, but it set me to thinking how right you are for each other. For I have no title or grand estate to offer in exchange for any affection you may wish to cast my way. I am a man of the law with rented rooms in my father's London house as of yesterday, where once I resided free of expense." Disconcertingly he suddenly moved toward the window, probably to be sure Rantchester had indeed left the street, but looked in the opposite direction to that of Rantchester's path."

"What is it?"

"I could have sworn Adam rode past." Leaning forward to obtain better view along the street to his right, he furthered with, "Not a glimpse of him. Pure imagination playing tricks no doubt." He turned, his eyes levelled to hers, searching as though still unsure of hers and Rantchester's relationship. "Adam heard today that he's unavoidably asset rich and cash poor, much to his chagrin. Lack of immediate finance is in part due to bequeathed monies to moi, which is sufficient to secure a substantial property here in London. And I have no idea why, but father bequeathed the horses, all, to my hands. And Caesar, until his last day, though I cannot fulfil that request. Needless to say, Adam is beside himself with rage."

Silence befell them for she could not think how to respond. Here was the man she held in great affection, and as good as telling her to wed another man. He was utterly convinced title, and status, were of prime importance to her. As for Adam penniless whilst in possession of vast assets, surely he would no doubt mortgage one or the other of his properties, though for how long such would keep him

111

solvent another matter entirely. But then, perhaps Eliza might curb his gambling ways by keeping him entertained in a manner befitting a stallion at stud.

A footman coughed, announcing his presence in the doorway, and said, "Dinner is now ready to be served, your ladyship."

"Thank you." As the footmen strode away Edwin returned to her side. She reached for his hand and clutched it to her breast, heart pounding. "What is a title and grand estate without love?"

"A life you are familiar with and one which I cannot provide for."

"If you think of me with tenderness in your heart, why seek to thrust me into the arms of another?"

"Because I think of you night and day, day and night. Thus intense anger within overwhelmed me out there in the street. I wanted to kill Rantchester for that kiss. A light kiss you claim which meant nothing to you. But don't you see. That precise incident caused me to think in terms of calling him out, and I know my skill with a blade is far superior to his. Such thoughts also afforded better understanding of what I believe may have caused Adam to commit heinous crimes. Proving such is a different matter. But jealousy, intense jealousy has been known to drive men to acts of insanity. The catalyst to my moment of insanity befell me out there in the street, being my love for you. I know my strengths and weaknesses, and I worry what I am capable of, what I might do if ever I felt you slipping from my grasp."

"Is that not normal for a man to feel protective of the one he loves? I too would be jealous if I thought your eye had strayed with earnest intent, and after seeing Adam and Eliza in gross intimacy, I am now better able to understand her feelings of contempt toward myself."

"Gross intimacy?"

"I shall enlighten you to part of what I witnessed, later, but for now we shall dine."

She led off, trailing him behind and not letting go of his hand even whilst ascending the staircase to the upper floor. "Oh, and just so that you know, I love you, too."

As they entered the dining room, she furthered, "Rantchester and I have a plan, a cunning plan. It may assist in getting Adam to confess to James' murder, and it would involve yourself and the Constable hiding in the hayloft at Abbeyfields. It was a doubtful plan beforehand, but now that you own the horses, we have a perfectly plausible reason to be in the mews at Abbeyfields" She placed a finger to her lips begging silence from him. "Later, let us enjoy dinner and no mention of Adam or Rantchester."

Eleven

It was dark, and it was humid.

She had no sense of time, and what had caused her to awaken so suddenly escaped her. There was nothing but silence of night, or so she had thought.

Unease gripped her, for sense of someone in the room caused a ripple of fear down her spine. There was a faint smell of hot wax and waft of candle smoke: the wick clearly extinguished quite recently. Perhaps the draft through the window left open to ease the overbearing atmosphere may have snuffed the flame.

She listened intently sure she could hear steady breathing. A man, it had to be a powerful man to her left, in the corner beyond the window and a good few strides from the door to her right. Nothing could she see, but neither could he, and even blindfolded she would know her way around the room.

Adam? Surely not. *How could he have gained entry to the house*? But as Rantchester had said, '*We are the last two people left alive who were present the night of James' death*'.

Sense of dread washed over her, and worse, lightning streaked across the sky and lit up the room. All but a fleeting glimpse a man seated in her chair confirmed her worst fears.

What to do?

To think was impossible when frozen with fear, but she must attempt to slip from the room unseen.

Poised ready to flee, she prayed for thunder. It came at first as a low rumble and by the time she had reached the

115

door an almighty crack of thunder shook the very foundations of the house.

She fled, snatched open the adjoining door to the room beyond, stepped inside, and slammed the door shut and locked it. Less familiar with the room she waited in hope of a lightning flash to light her way to the bed. When lightening streaked the sky and lit the path ahead she sped across the room, and with the bed reached she worked her hands along its edge.

How was it possible for men to sleep through a thunderstorm?

Upon reaching the head of the bed she felt for pillows, and then reached out her hand in hope of locating Edwin's shoulder: nothing.

She stretched further across the bed: and still nothing. She felt around the centre of the bed. He was gone, and abandonment overwhelmed her.

Fool, what a fool she had been to suppose he would stay when assured she was safe in her bedchamber. He had so disapproved of her suggesting he stay the night in the adjoining room, and had argued it was fitting if he slept at the far end of the corridor in one of the bedchambers beyond her late grandfather's. How silly, for had she asked the same of Rantchester he would have stayed without question, her safety more important than protecting her honour.

Which room then had Edwin settled to?

She dared not venture out into the corridor, for the slamming of the adjoining door would have alerted the intruder to her flight, though with luck he would assume her to be making her way toward the servants' quarters, for where else could she seek help.

There was nothing for it but to clamber into the bed, and hope someone stomping about the house would alert the servants. First though it was imperative to make her way to the outer door and turn the key to the lock position. Oh how she wished herself more familiar with her father's old room, but it was not a place where a child had dared venture unless invited. She had not entered it that often since his passing, whereas her mother's room had become her bedchamber, and her parents' former private rooms across the corridor hers, too. Though in truth, the house was now that of the new Duke's.

She felt along the side of the bed and slid to her knees at its foot. It was safest to crawl, and vague memory of furniture and where placed around the room proved of little help, but a hand extended now and then was her best means in avoidance of colliding with a chair, stool, or occasional table. Her fine lawn nightgown impeded any sense of dignified crawl and necessitated its raising, twisting and tucking-in, and utterly immodest she carried on her way feeling ahead as she went.

Almost at where she believed the door was situated her heart stalled, for light appeared slightly to her right indicating the foot of the door. She held her breath, and sure enough she could hear the latch handle as it was pressed downward. The door opened and light from a candle progressed into the room.

"Georgette, are you in here?" came at her in a hushed manly whisper.

"Yes," her whispered reply, whilst scrabbling to disengage her nightgown from her hips. "Where were you?"

Edwin chuckled, a low husky chuckle, his candle held her way and her thighs still exposed and nightgown impossibly knotted. "It was me, in your room, asleep in the chair."

"You; in the chair? You scared me half to death."

117

He came to her, lowered himself to one knee, and placed the candlestick on the floor.

"Here, let me help."

His chosen attire although amusing, his knee bared and chest exposed, she asked: "What is that thing you have about your waist?"

"The coverlet from the bed," his reply, hands drifting to her knotted nightgown. "It was all that came to hand, for it was a spur of the moment decision on my part to come and look in on you."

"Why?"

"I don't know. I couldn't get to sleep and felt uneasy. I just needed to be sure you were safe."

"As you can see, I am quite safe, despite scared witless."

The back of his hand brushed against her thigh and where in broad daylight she might have blushed at the thrill of his touch, the shadow of candlelight thankfully served purpose as a liberating mask.

He chuckled, a familiar chuckle. "I sat in your chair delighting in watching over you as you slept, and likewise drifted into oblivion. A damn thunderclap woke me and the candle had snuffed and then a door in the room slammed shut. By the time I located the tinderbox and relit the candle you were gone. You weren't in the corridor so I looked in here first."

Thoughts and feelings never encountered before dispatched a quicksilver shiver of shameful lust the length of her spine, more so as he finally disentangled her nightgown and regained his feet.

In that brief movement he shrouded a vital part of himself in haste, for mutual excitement was quite evident and neither could deny it nor hide it from each other. Upon his extending a hand and hauling her up from the floor she leaned into him, eager to engage in a kiss and to nestle against his chest.

He kissed her the like she had longed for since his snatched kiss at a kissing gate in Wells, but this time it would not be so easy to step back and go their separate ways nor did she want to. She savoured the feel of his body against hers, his lips on hers, the sparring with tongues and his arms embracing. With anyone else closeness such as this would terrify her in fear it would go too far, as happened on several occasions in her past when men had taken her flirty tease as open invitation. With him she wanted that, wanted him to go far, wanted him to take her, to make her his alone.

He relinquished his hold, hand held firm against his groin to shield his predicament, its presence made known to her throughout the kiss. "You have to leave, Georgette. Now, and no argument, for restraint of mind and abstention from physical pleasure is a man's worst nightmare, more so when a woman wanton in pursuit of affection happens to be in his bedchamber. It is torture indeed."

"I cannot, and will not go back into my room. I don't know why but I no longer feel safe in this house. The thought of Adam out there, somewhere, and the not knowing where, terrifies me. I fear for Rantchester's safety, too. He quite believes he will one day be faced with murderous thugs along some dark alley, and we; he and I, are the only living souls who were there on that fatal—"

"It's all right, my love, I concede to us remaining here together, but a sheet between us is not enough. I have to get dressed in breeches at least."

"If a sheet and nightgown are not enough, then we are lost in any case. And what difference, may I ask, will breeches make?"

119

"You tempt the very devil from within, and breeches, believe it, will save us both from any likelihood of embarrassment."

She sighed. "I shall turn my back until you are safe between sheet and blanket, will that do?"

"If you insist, then I shall away to the bed."

She dutifully turned her back, eyes alighting on a dressing mirror atop a chest. His reflection therein became an amusing sight, and when he drew the coverlet from around his waist and scattered it across the bed, there he was in all his naked glory. *How could any woman avert her eyes from such exquisite male beauty*? When dressed he was of stylish cut, his height striking, handsome of face and grey eyes arresting. Now, in candlelight, his body seemed less lean than imagined yet taut, his thighs muscular and she could well understand his need to clad himself in decent manner.

As soon as his breeches were affixed, she asked, "Can I turn round now?"

"You can come to bed."

She did and clambered in, and tested to see if he had indeed placed himself above the sheet and beneath the coverlet. "A truer gentleman I could not find."

Chuckles ensued, for he was head already to pillow, hands clasped behind his head. "You thought I wouldn't?"

"Oh I quite believed your word to be that of a gentleman."

"Even so, if discovered like this, how do we explain ourselves?"

"To whom? Servants? We are to all intents and purposes alone, Edwin, entirely alone."

"Exactly, and the sheet stays where it is." He let fall his arm behind her back. "Come here, snuggle up and get some sleep."

120

She did as bid, luxuriating in sense of togetherness and the feel of his protective arm about her. He kissed her head, a reassuring hug given and she listened to his breathing and steady beat of his heart and sensed the moment he slipped into slumber. She closed her eyes rather glad he had left the candle burning, though daybreak would be upon them within a few hours. *What then*?

Twelve

He was deeply, madly, in love.

For two nights they had shared the same bed, a sheet between them, and for two nights her body beside him had plagued the very devil within. Despite inner needs and desires, he knew Georgette was genuinely scared, not only for herself, but for Rantchester, too.

To take advantage of her need for reassurance and comfort was unthinkable, desire nonetheless difficult to keep at bay. There was little he could do to lessen her fears, and as much as he wanted her, had wanted to make love to her, she would thankfully be on her way back to Bath tomorrow and temptingly out of his reach.

With Rantchester sleeping two rooms distant and the new duke across the corridor, she had agreed to remain in her own room. A creaking door or floorboard in the night could perchance be overheard, whereas in daylight there was much ado about a house and inconsequential sounds passed unnoticed.

Although he now missed having her in his arms he relished freedom between sheets and no damn breeches to impede comfort of movement.

He leaned toward his candle and snuffed the flame with a spittle-wet finger and thumb, and fell back to the pillows. All but a moment or two and he couldn't be sure if imagination had taken hold, or that he had heard the click of a door catch. He listened intently for sounds in his room, the corridor, and beyond, but there was nothing. The house was silent. He closed his eyes, for with two other men in the house and both capable of putting up a good defence if

123

called upon to do so, plus his own swordstick beside the bed, Georgette had protection aplenty.

He woke with a start, and conscious of movement in the bed beside him he turned toward her, because no one else would be sneaking into his bed, thus he whispered, "You shouldn't be here."

"I know, but I couldn't sleep."

Tentatively he reached out his hand hoping against hope she'd slipped between blankets and sheet, but she hadn't and his fingers collided with fine lawn nightgown barely covering her thigh. He withdrew his hand. "Wait, we can't sleep like this."

She ignored his comment and slid closer, and slipped her arm across his bare midriff and snuggled up against him. "I'm here now. Go back to sleep."

"Sleep? You expect me to sleep?" he said, in a hushed tone. "No, Georgette, we cannot do this. I can't do this."

"What difference does it make whether we have a sheet between us or not?"

"You really need me to explain the consequences of our sleeping together, and of a woman lying alongside with nothing but a fine nightgown to protect her from possible embarrassment of male desires?"

"Of course not, but I trust you, implicitly."

"Georgette, my sweet darling, no matter how much I may try to remain impartial to your charms, whilst you in all innocence snuggle to my body, there's a part of my anatomy that has a mind all its own and might well make its presence known to you."

"I am aware of that, and if it does so be it."

He drew breath, all his senses on alert, and he knew, knew he was in trouble. There was sweet essence of lavender, sweet essence of woman, her hair brushing his shoulder, her lips on his as though her catlike green eyes could see in the dark. It was utter torture, utter torture, and she had to know what effect it was having upon him. She could not help but feel his ardour, know it for what it was, yet she came closer still, letting it nuzzle into the cleft of her. Her fine lawn gown was a barrier, yes, but so thin barely noticeable. He could feel the heat of her, knew her to be savouring his arousal; swelling and pressing against her.

Damn it, he could resist all he wanted in desperation to be the perfect gentleman, but when a woman kisses a man and incites his ardour there comes the moment of must have, must achieve the ultimate. He wanted that, oh God how he wanted that.

But *did she want it too? Was this all tease, and then, if he took control, would she panic?*

To kiss her was bliss, and he drew her into his arms, and if nothing else he would have part of her, and pleasure her. If she wanted him, truly wanted him, he might oblige if absolutely sure she was ready to embrace him as any man would desire of her.

He slid his hand beneath the covers, and gently drew her nightgown up across her thighs and sought a breast. Her softness cupped to hand seemed to please her, for she too sought to caress his chest, his stomach, but her hand drifting ever downward and her fingers seeking his ardour for herself caused agony the like he hadn't experienced in a long while.

He sensed nervousness, as though afraid she had ventured too far, for she pulled back a little.

He ceased kissing her, and whispered, "You don't have to do this, and if you want to go back to your own room, I am happy for that to happen."

"I'm not afraid of you, Edwin. I want to be here. I want you to make love to me, but I am afraid that if you do you will think badly of me, think me shameful and then never want to marry me."

"If we choose to love one another as man and wife before we're wed," he said, letting his hand glide from her breast across her taught tummy to the cleft of her thighs. "I won't love you any the less, but I suggest a marriage be sooner rather than later." He caressed her soft inner self, and dipped his fingers into the moist sanctuary of aroused woman. "This is only the beginning of the pleasure we shall share for all time."

A soft whispering laugh preceded, "You tease in a most delightful way."

"You think my attentions delightful then let me delight you even more."

He shuffled down the bed and before she could protest, he had his lips deployed to the pearl of her womanhood. She squirmed and writhed beneath onslaught of his tongue, and he sensed her efforts in fighting the need to cry out, and all too soon ecstasy overwhelmed her. She fell to trembles and quakes fists thrashing the bed, and it was the moment, the moment for him to test her willingness to let him make love to her in full manly glory. But he had to be sure; absolute sure she was ready for the ultimate.

To creep atop her was heaven, his mouth to hers, and whilst kissing her deeply he dipped a finger inside of her. Where she might have shrunk away, he sensed her enjoyment. She wanted him, no doubt about it, and with gentle approach he nestled his burgeoned self against her

126

and slipped into her moistness with ease. There was momentary resistance. He withdrew a fraction, and once again slid forward and this time thrust in his desire to have her blossom to him. A little gasp of surprise escaped her lips, and he eased back a little, but she was his now, and he hers.

He savoured the moment, loved the feel of her cloaked about him, loved moving within her, and whispered, "Wicked temptress."

"The thought of you as slave to my whims, wicked indeed."

She writhed her hips she rose to meet him, and it was all too damn special, too thrilling, too much to bear, and he could hold back no longer. The agony and ecstasy of it all brought him to the brink of man deriving utmost gratification from woman, and as much as he wanted to let go seed of man it would be unfair, unjust before marriage. He withdrew.

It was time to depart from London, and although it grieved her to leave the London house, she felt her duty was fully done as laid down by her grandfather. She could not fault its new owner. She quite believed Lieutenant Rufus Meredith would see right by his inheritance. Without doubt he was a man of honour, of goodly reputation in military circles, and despite his demeanour that of a hardened naval officer, it was somewhat of a surprise to learn his charming manner had not, as yet, begotten him a wife.

"Are we now ready to leave, Georgette?" enquired Rantchester.

"We are," her reply, eyes alighting on Rufus in conversation with Edwin. "I hope the weather holds, for it looks a little overcast."

"We shall be cosy enough," said Rantchester, a broad smile. He then turned and intervened in the manly exchange, alerting the two men to her imminent departure.

Rufus stepped forward, caught up her hand and cupped it between his. "Please, when paying visit to London, use this house as if it is yours. For morally, it is as much yours as it shall ever be mine, so too that of the Martcham Estate."

"You are most kind, your Grace."

"Rufus, call me Rufus," said he, his dark chestnut eyes entreating trust from her.

She had not thought family resemblance could be so strong given his distant relationship, but he was most definitely that of the male Beaumont bloodline despite his being a Meredith. He bore the sharp-featured handsomeness of her grandfather and father alike, slight of body and of good height.

"Then I am Georgette to you, and I shall scold you rotten if you dare to call me Lady Beaumont."

A hearty chuckle resonated with affection. "Will you come and stay at Martcham, when I am there? I would like that. We are family after all, and there is much to learn about a family I never knew I had a week past."

"Write to me, and I shall write you all that I know of the Beaumont family as far back as I have knowledge of."

"It will please me greatly to oblige in your request." He bowed then, and stepped back. "God speed and safe journey."

Rantchester made toward the door held wide by a footman, Rufus followed, which left her and Edwin face to face. There was still so much she wanted to say, their intimacy the previous night unforgettable, wonderful and she wanted to embrace him, kiss him, to have his arms about her. But she couldn't, and for sake of respectability that very morning, he'd made her depart his room at daybreak and no time since for a moment alone, until now.

"You will let me know when you are to return to Abbeyfields, will you not?" enquired she.

"That I will, and I shall arrange for the dinner party as suggested by Rantchester, when I know Adam and Eliza are for sure in residence." He stepped closer, caught up her hand and whispered, "I love you, and don't ever forget that, no matter what passes between now and when we can be together again." He kissed her fingers, let fall her hand, his eyes not leaving hers for a second his voice once again most formal. "I shall call upon you, Lady Beaumont, as soon as able."

He proffered his arm, she accepted and they walked toward the door. "I look forward to that, and to all your news."

Without further ado, and although her heart fell leaden at leaving him behind, once seated in the carriage and Rufus out of earshot Edwin said to Rantchester. "Look after her for on your head be it if harm should befall Georgette."

Rantchester matched him. "That I shall do, with pleasure and honour. Though what we have in mind, when the time comes, is dangerous, indeed. God forbid we place her in worse danger than before."

"We will be two against one, and I am not the least bit intimidated by my brother."

Why must they talk as though she was absent?

"It was part my idea Edwin, and yes, I will be a little nervous about it all, but I will be alert to any unpleasant eventuality."

129

"That may be so, angel," said Rantchester, "but I have the notion the Datchett girl must never be dismissed as a harmless female."

"Nor I," said Edwin. "For although a drover thought he heard a young man in argument with my father the day of his murder, Eliza's voice could easily be mistaken for that of a young male."

"True enough, dear fellow, and a vicious whip hand doth that woman have when out hunting."

Edwin's hand fell brief to hers. "Be careful, and be safe."

With that he closed the door of the carriage and waved farewell, and almost immediately it gave a little jolt and then rolled forward. They were on their way back to Bath, the coach protecting them from the probability of foul weather en route.

All her belongings from the London house were destined to follow in a few days, and Rufus had declined her proposal to leave her grandfather's carriage and team of four for his use. He was adamant he preferred riding to saddle, and until such time as he found himself a bride he had no use for a carriage, so that too would be coming to Bath. Quite sure he was being overly generous in refusing her kind offer she decided to accept his word, and no more to be said.

Thirteen

She could not have been more nervous.

"We have to do this Georgette," said Rantchester, a re-assuring smile. "We must to all intents and purposes appear as though enchanted by each other."

"In *love*. We have to convince Adam we're in *love*, not merely attracted to each other."

She linked her arm through his and snuggled closer, albeit the open carriage was rumbling along the drive to Monkton Abbeyfields, they might well be spied on approach if Adam was keening their arrival. One glance at her companion, and she spilled her thoughts:

"I don't suppose Beatrice and Ranulph are looking forward to this dinner party, one bit. And why, why did Adam rearrange today's events at short notice? It is somewhat disquieting, do you not agree?"

"Odd indeed, and may well scupper our previous plan."

"But we can still look at the horses, for that is why you were supposedly invited by Edwin in hope you might purchase one or two."

"I do believe we are under scrutiny. See the window to the far left of the ground floor?" said Rantchester, as the carriage approached the front of Monkton Abbeyfelds. "We must let events take their course and hope we may yet succeed in our aims."

The old house towered above them its prior monastic aura implying sanctuary and a place of meditation rather than a place of evil cunning and despicable practices, but that is what it had become. It was a hellish place in which Ranulph had suffered cruelty the like she could not have

131

imagined, and if not for Edwin and Rantchester's presence, she would not be venturing there at all.

Rantchester alighted from the carriage and assisted in her descent with an overtly loving attentiveness, and strange as it seemed to have agreed to a romantic charade, she was truly glad of his arm to hold on to. Every step took them closer to Adam, but it was Eliza who awaited them in the grand hall.

She could not help but feel Ranulph truly had captured Eliza's witch persona; her raven hair and widow's peak, her dark crow-like eyes and mouth grim-tight. She was also much taller than memory afforded from a first sighting on *The Chapter House* steps.

"Welcome to Monkton Abbeyfields," said Eliza, her voice as deep as Ranulph's. "Follow me." She immediately spun on her heels, her fine purple coloured silk gown adding to her dourness, her bonnet black with purple feather. "Come," she said, not missing a step in stride, nor pausing to say, "Lord Brockenbury awaits in the library."

The library? Why the library?

Rantchester squeezed her hand as though sensing her apprehension, a reassuring gesture of togetherness, though not a word uttered.

Upon entry to the library, her heart dived on first sighting Adam, and soared at the sight of Edwin.

Ranulph and Beatrice were looking most unhappy.

"Rantchester, old boy, good to have you back at Abbeyfields," said Adam, striding forward. "And Georgette, sweet, sweet, Georgette."

Adam caught up her hand and thankfully her gloves protected flesh from his vile mouth whilst he planted a kiss upon her knuckles. "Come now, Rantchester, you cannot keep her all to yourself."

132

Adam's arm proffered was the last thing she wished to oblige, but nonetheless slipped her arm from Rantchester's and linked with Adam. "There, just like old times. I shall now take you on a grand tour of the house, and you shall see the improvements I have made since becoming lord in residence."

She assumed the others were to attend too, but a quick glance at Eliza suggested otherwise: shock etched on the other woman's face.

Adam's proposed grand tour clearly had not been broached prior to their arrival, and the last thing she wanted was to be left alone with Adam, and said, "Would it not be better for Miss Datchett to afford us ladies a tour of the house, after all, it is a womanly thing to do."

Edwin then said, "Georgette is right. The marquis is here essentially on horse business. And, if you recall, you agreed all the stable staff and farm hands could attend the local stock fair this afternoon as a reward for good service to father."

Eliza joined with Edwin in attempt to scupper Adam's proposal. "I doubt very much the men will return before nightfall."

Adam let slip her arm from his grasp. "Very well, the grand tour can wait until later." He turned to face her, and despite his seeming pleasant personae the old Adam lurked in the depths of his eyes, and she knew for sure she would never be safe if left alone in his company. His response was bitter toned. "It would seem the horses are of greater priority."

"You are fond of horses, are you not, Lady Beaumont?" enquired Edwin.

"I am, and would love to see the horses, too."

Adam turned about in brusque manner. "Then let us proceed to the stable yard, for the sooner those damn beasts are gone from my property the better." He turned to Edwin. "The end of the week, I want the lot gone by then, for I shall purchase horses to my own tastes."

Edwin bowed; his tone sardonic. "You seriously require use of all the stalls by week's end?"

Adam's eyes flashed erring malice. "Whether I do or not is of no concern of yours. Now let us get this over and done with."

"Should you not stay here with Lady Beaumont and Miss Knight, the horses are Edwin's not yours," suggested Eliza, seeming keen to keep the ladies confined to the house, and Adam within her sights. "It's very hot today."

"I'll do as I please. "Adam looked a little annoyed but nonetheless conceded to Eliza. "See to it, then. See the ladies refreshed." With that he turned to the men. "Shall we go?"

"There is no need for my presence here," snapped Eliza, linking her arm in Adam's. "I might as well come with you, for we have servants for the menial tasks. It's not as if Lady Beaumont is without company."

Although rather amused by Eliza's swift action of taking Adam's arm, Georgette's eyes settled on the man in possession of her own heart, and even though they had to appear as distant acquaintances, she duly addressed Edwin. "I have paddocks aplenty and adequate stabling at Hazelgrove, Mr. Brockenbury. I will gladly accommodate your horses for as long as need be."

Adam faltered in step, and said, "Accommodate Edwin's horses?" He laughed a deprecating laugh. "Whatever for? He has precious little time for equestrian pursuits and you'll surely find yourself left to provide for his confounded animals in more ways than one. His time in London with his mistress is of far greater importance."

Mistress, what mistress?

She could not let Adam see his words had hurt her, and she said, "I feel sure your brother and I can come to an amicable arrangement."

To the occasion rose Rantchester with a chuckle. "Mistress, eh? Well I'll be damned." He slapped Edwin on the shoulder, a sly wink for good measure in passing. "Then let me relieve you of equine binding ties to this part of the world."

Rantchester caught up her arm, grinned, and although she knew his comment to be a ploy, Beatrice' looked concerned along with Ranulph, for they both knew of hers and Edwin's love for each other. As they all filed out to the stable yard, she too pondered Adam's proclamation and whether she had made a fool of herself in clambering into Edwin's bed if he indeed had a mistress.

With small talk kept alive by Rantchester, Adam and Eliza strode ahead in utter silence. She could hear Ranulph and Edwin in exchange but they were walking at a discreet distance behind.

By the time they had reached the stable yard it became obvious Ranulph and Beatrice had decided to turn back for Edwin came striding onward alone. He stopped to speak with Ranulph's driver, who, after quick inspection of harness urged the pair of bright bays onward and Ranulph's barouche rolled out of the yard.

Rantchester's men in conversation with Ranulph's looked on in wonder, perhaps thinking they too were about to be called upon to whisk their master away. Edwin did indeed speak with them but only to suggest they might like to go to the house kitchens for refreshments. With their charges unhitched and already tethered to rails surrounding a paddock, and hay aplenty in racks, the men set off in pursuit of reward. For they had a long wait ahead, their services required post dinner.

135

As Edwin drew level Adam cast Eliza from his arm and said, "Was the cripple not up to the walk?"

"Must you refer to Ranulph in that obnoxious term?" said Edwin, a glower that caused her heart to falter for it was cold, his eyes murderous.

Was his response due to his elder brother's callousness or earlier mention of a mistress?

Undaunted by Adam's vile tongue, Edwin furthered with: "Ranulph sends his regards but as Beatrice was feeling a little unwell, they decided it was best to return to Fenemore."

Adam shook his head as though disbelieving a word said, "What pretty Miss Knightley sees in the cripple is beyond me, and God help any offspring to come from that match."

She quite thought Edwin was about to lunge at Adam, but Rantchester set immediate precedence for horse banter. "Right, which equines are you keen to be rid of?"

"This way," replied Edwin, gesturing for Rantchester to enter the inner sanctum of the stable mews. "Two excellent hunters if you're interested, and there's a youngster that's exceedingly fleet of foot. He may make for a good race horse."

The two men strode off down the interior corridor, stalls to their right stretching the full length of the building. She stopped to collapse her parasol in readiness to keep close to Edwin, for memories of what had occurred in the hayloft in the past, and now lying overhead, caused a shiver of fear to ripple down her spine. She had to step inside the mews and could not let what had happened to James prevent her from staying calm and collected, for Adam's eyes were upon her.

She turned and strolled along the corridor not wishing to impinge on the men's conversation, but Adam soon caught up with her.

"Eliza has gone back to the house to see my little brother and his lady love off the premises. Isn't that nice of her?" He proffered his arm. "Can we be friends, Georgette? I really would like for us all to be friends." He chuckled, but it was far from hearty and honest in its presentation. "I never thought Rantchester would steal your heart, and can't say as I'm wholly convinced he has."

Rantchester and Edwin had stopped at a stall half way along the corridor, and Edwin reached for a leather halter as she said:

"Rupert and I discovered we had much in common, and mutual respect for one another is vital for good companionship. Love was therefore inevitable in the circumstance of like minds."

Adam paused, causing her to falter mid-step. His eyes levelled on hers bearing malevolence, his visage a mask of contempt. "A marriage of convenience it is to be then, and rank for rank of your stepping back into society head held high as a marchioness?" He laughed, heartily laughed. "Rantchester, you've been had, dear fellow. This lady no more loves you than I that Datchett bitch."

Silence descended and time seemed suspended.

Rantchester and Edwin looked one to the other, for a scream came from behind and Eliza seemed to fly at Adam. "You and her, it has always been you and her."

Adam turned to face Eliza. His expression suddenly that of shock and horror as Eliza thrust upward with a two-pronged pitchfork into his upper torso.

Edwin rushed forward, but Eliza fled and slammed the door shut and rammed home the outer bolt. Not that it mattered they still had exit by way of the coach house.

"Get this out of me," said Adam. He stumbled backwards grappling with the handle of the pitchfork desperate to wrench it free from his body. Blood trickled

137

from the corner of his mouth and with tremendous strength and air of madness about him he extracted the pitchfork. "I'll kill that bitch, so help me I'll shoot the bitch." But his knees crumpled, his expression that of resignation to his fate. "Damn her to hell and back." Every breath taken and every word spoken came forth in blooded gurgles. "I am of mind—she's done for me."

Rantchester came alongside, said, "Hell's waiting dear fellow, might as well confess all and go in good heart."

Adam collapsed, said: "I'll see you in hell, first." There was no doubting he would die and nothing could be done for him.

Edwin returned and knelt beside Adam, and cradled the head of his dying brother against his thigh. "What would you have me do?"

In a blood-choked whisper, Adam said, "See that bitch hangs."

A faint cough escaped Adam, his breathing less noticeable until finally nothing.

Edwin glanced at Rantchester and shook his head. As he carefully lowered Adam flat to the floor, one large door of the coach house was heard to slam shut.

Rantchester turned and ran the length of the corridor to the coach house, but the second outer door was slammed before he could reach it; the securing bar heard clanging into place.

There was light from barred windows but no way out.

Rantchester then yelled, "She's set a fire in here."

They would all perish, and fear the like she had never experienced before overwhelmed Georgette.

Fourteen

Set fire to the coach house? Why? Why would Eliza do that?

Smoke had begun drifting through the doorway, and Edwin and Rantchester with coats wrenched from their shoulders beat at flames flaring from hay pushed beneath and behind a coach.

Their efforts proved fruitless. The coach was soon alight and flames from its canopy reached the ceiling above. "I'm going aloft," said Edwin, making for the loft stairs. "There's a way to get out up there."

Rantchester threw his badly burned jacket away and caught her arm. "Back, we have to go back."

Once they were back in the corridor he closed the inner door, but the horses were restless, fear in their eyes. The stalls were fogged with smoke and more seeping through gaps around the door. Rantchester searched the tack room in hope of finding something to batter the far door, but nothing came to hand, and instead he tried to shoulder it but it wouldn't budge.

The hayloft had caught fire, the crackling sound terrifying. Half choking and fearing the worst, she felt sure they would soon be dead alongside Adam, and then the door was suddenly opened and in came Edwin.

"Out Georgette, out to a safe distance but stay where I can see you. Rantchester get some air in your lungs, get your horses into the paddock and I'll get these horses out."

She rushed outside, gulped air, coughed, and gulped more air. Oh God, the hayloft was ablaze all the way along the top of the stalls. Presumably Edwin had shimmied down the rope left dangling from an overhead pull-wheel.

139

Rantchester coughed and coughed but hurried away to do as
bid in setting his horses free from their tethers. She couldn't leave, for she could hear the horses within the mews, their frantic cries heart-rending, and so panicked Edwin needed help.

About to go back inside to assist she was forced to step aside, for Edwin appeared; leading a horse by its halter. He held it firm despite its frenzied attempts to break free. He then let slip the halter from its head when the equine was sensibly facing in the right direction.

"It has to be one at a time," he said, before rushing back inside.

There were six horses to save, she knew that much, and he couldn't possibly get them all out before the whole building would be consumed by fire. Rantchester came back still coughing, and in passing said, "My men, at the house. *Go*." He then followed in Edwin's footsteps.

It was true she was better out of the way, her gown impractical for leading horses to safety in a hurry, but there were footmen in the house as well as Rantchester's men.

Why had no one else seen or smelt the smoke?

She hitched up her skirts, turned and ran from the stable yard back through the walled garden to the house. The garden doors were open and as she ran through the drawing room she called out in hope someone would hear, but no one answered.

Where were the footmen?

She hurried toward the east wing to the kitchens, and there found them so engrossed in chatter and laughter with Rantchester's men and housemaids no one noticed her enter.

"*Fire*," she screamed, "there's a terrible fire in the stable yard."

Silence befell the room but momentary, and then men flooded past her. One of the maids said, "Is you all right yer ladyship? You do look right pale, and yer lovely pink gown be all ruined."

One of Rantchester's men returned, said, "Cloths, I need big drying cloths."

A maid nearby didn't ask why, she gathered several from a drawer and handed them over. As he left she followed, so too the maids and as they all ran he shook the drying cloths free from neat folds en route.

As soon as they reached the stable yard he tossed all the drying cloths into a water trough, and retrieved them soaking wet. He didn't falter upon seeing flames licking around doorposts and pieces of blazing timber falling from the roof trusses: he sped into the mews.

Unable to see Rantchester's driver and groom, she presumed they had already entered the blazing mews. Rantchester came out with a horse, and it was so terrified it looked as though he might not be able to hold onto it. But with a footman's help they led it safe to the paddock. Almost immediately another horse appeared with a wet cloth over its head, and although quite obviously tense it nonetheless trotted away in hand as opposed to dragging its handlers to the paddock.

Rantchester's driver appeared next with a magnificent dark bay its head shrouded, but at that very moment the roof of the coach house collapsed. The horse reared up on its hindquarters and unable to hold it the coachman let it go of its own free will and it sped after the previous horse. As it did so, the hayloft roof started to collapse. She drew breath fearing the worst, her stomach colliding with heart.

She assumed the next horse was the last horse for it came through the door as though the very devil was on its heel, smoke billowing around it. Rantchester's man turned

141

it toward the paddock and let the poor thing take flight. He paused, drew several deep breaths and once again rushed back inside.

Where was Edwin?

Merely moments seemed an eternity and then he and Rantchester's man stepped forth with Adam's body. Her heart reached out to him, for face and clothes blackened Edwin looked weary as Adam's body was placed beside the gateway to the walled garden.

He searched the gathered, no words needed upon their eyes meeting. It was as though he needed to be sure everyone was safe and accounted for, and then he turned to a footman. What was said she could not hear, nor the footman's reply but Rantchester's man intervened and a serious exchange ensued as they all surveyed the building; the billowing smoke and flames leaping ever skyward.

With the coach house and stalls gone, two carriages and Adam's curricle, so too valuable harness and tack were lost along with stable staff accommodation. But due to the direction of a light breeze the fire had not spread to the barn or the looseboxes across the yard, where she and the maids were standing at a safe distance.

The maids chattered and whispered upon spying Adam's demise and snippets of enlightenment drifted her way.

Was it any wonder Adam was the cause of their revelations?

She was not the least surprised to hear he had entertained immoral advances toward the maids, some of whom had left under mysterious circumstances.

But where was Eliza?

That was something she wished to know, for one maid said she thought she had seen her run into the house through the front entrance and rush up the stairs.

Was she still there?

Rantchester came to her side as the maids began drifting away, and said, "Damnable business, and what now one may ask?"

"I presume the Constable will have to be notified as to what has happened as soon as possible. Though it would have been far better had he accompanied us here this day."

"It was our bad luck he was due in court this day," said Rantchester, glancing about. "What of the Datchette girl?"

"I was thinking the very same thing, but according to a maid she's at the house. Presumably in her bedchamber."

"Her horse is gone."

"Is it?"

Rantchester inclined his head to a loosebox; the door left wide open. "It was there when we arrived, and is now gone."

"Then she may not be at the house at all. Perchance she fled to her bedchamber to change into riding apparel. She could be well away from here by now."

"Best find out, and the sooner the better." He strode across to Edwin, as three footmen set off back to the house with Adam's body. "The Datchette girl may well have made a run for it on horseback."

Edwin spun round eyes to the loosebox. "Where can she go? Without Adam's say so she cannot draw on ready monies, and cannot be so mad as to believe she's a victim, surely. Dear God, what have we done this day?"

"We foresaw none of this, dear fellow," intoned Rantchester, his face as sooty black as any chimney sweep. "I agree we set the scene for orchestrated conflict within the stable yard, our intentions honourable enough, if woefully naïve in assumption Adam would ever confess to his sins. Damn it all, even in death throes he thought only of revenge."

143

"What have I ever done to deserve such injustice?" Edwin cast his eyes skyward. "A dead brother and now his title and responsibilities have fallen to my shoulders, of which I neither want, nor any part of this evil place. And Eliza, what to do about the girl? The Constable has to be informed. Yet I feel some sympathy toward her. She was but a means unto financial gain for my brother and their intended marriage, as father stated, madness indeed. He swore they would wed over his dead body, and such would not have come to pass if not for Adam's rancorous outburst."

Rantchester said, "Are you saying you are no longer of mind she murdered your father? We both know she could pass as a young man in voice, and the way in which she administered that pitchfork, insanity prevailed, did it not?"

Edwin shook his head as though the enormity of it all weighed too heavy. "Life can be cruel in so many ways, and Eliza's very existence is a story in itself, poor girl. What could be expected of one begotten by a daughter and father? My father always said his sister would forever be damned for hopping to their father's bed the way in which she did and no shame about her."

"I dare say it happens more that we shall ever know, though bad form when a man beds his daughter instead of bedding the servant gals." Rantchester attempted to brush sooty deposits from his shirtsleeves: a pointless exercise. "For the life of me I cannot recall being this filthy, not even as a child." He glanced at the still smouldering building. "What shall you do, rebuild the mews?"

"The house requires a coach house, so yes, rebuild as soon as possible, though I have no wish to reside here."

"Not live here? It's a sizable seat and good farmland."

"I despised the place as a child, and even now, I feel as

though evil forces are at play, toying with my life as though I am their puppet to tease, to torture and destroy at a given whim."

Rantchester's expression turned grave. "I grant a sinister element to Monkton Abbeyfields has always existed and splendidly suited to Adam and Eliza's secretive pursuits. But where shall you live if not here?"

"Now that I am officially a circuit judge for the West Country, anywhere will do just fine and this place can be put to rental." Edwin glanced her way, and further said, "I shall be called upon to sit in London too, and father's house there will serve me well."

"Your house, Lord Brockenbury," said Rantchester, a chuckle, "and whether you be gowned in red or not, the title sits well on your shoulders."

"I earned my judicial colours, whereas the Brockenbury lordship has been foisted on me by Eliza." He reached for Georgette's hand and drew it to his lips. "Are you sure you still wish to engage with this Brockenbury, now that you know madness is endemic within our bloodlines?"

Rantchester laughed, said, "Mad, yes, in not having asked her to marry you whilst in London." He slapped Edwin on the back in passing and called back over his shoulder. "I shall ask for her hand if you don't."

"He's jesting," she said, a smile, "and although I owe him much he expects only friendship in return. He knows my heart is yours."

"Is that so?" said Edwin, his hands slipping about her waist. "And will you, will you wed this man, whose bed you clambered into most wilful and wanton?"

"If you agree to clamber into mine tonight, for I fear I will not sleep knowing Eliza might come calling. I think her revengeful nature runs deep, very deep indeed."

His lips embraced tender light, his grip upon her relinquished in a thrice and quite understandable given the circumstances of his brother's death. "I shall oblige in your request, but will need to return here at first light." He caught up her hand, held it firm in his clasp. "I must now see to matters most unpleasant, and think it best if Rantchester were to return you home right away."

They set off back to the house hands clasped her heart tumbling over itself for Edwin had agreed to come to her that night. She would not be alone and yet— "How, how will you come to Hazel Grove, when you have no carriage nor a saddle to your name?"

"I shall be with you before nightfall, have no fear." He squeezed her hand in a reassuring gesture. "Father had me astride a pony as soon as I had my feet, and by five years of age I could jump that pony over poles without a saddle. So getting to Hazel Grove on a horse will be child's play."

"Yes but you were a child back then."

"Believe it, I will not fail you."

Fifteen

She was at home, albeit alone, but assured Edwin would arrive before dark. Rantchester had dutifully departed for home directly after dinner, and she was feeling relatively safe, for her staff consisted of two footmen and her personal maid from her grandfather's London house. Although the kitchen staff and house maids were all local and new to her and new to Hazel Grove House, nonetheless, all were conscientious in every task undertaken.

The footmen as instructed by Rantchester had secured all windows and doors at ground level, and with supper of hot chocolate consumed she watched from her drawing room window as twilight descended to darkness without. Edwin had promised to be with her by nightfall, and she could not help but feel something had happened to detain him. True enough Rantchester had stopped off at the Constable's residence on behalf of Edwin, and the Constable had said '*the murder victim is going nowhere, while the murderess at large will be priority for the morrow*'.

And so, Georgette was now left standing in a candlelit room and as good as in the dark to happenings beyond the periphery of her own land.

She could stay below stairs and hope Edwin would arrive soon, or retire aloft and fret his absence from above. She chose the latter.

At least from her bedchamber window she could enjoy the sweet scents of summer flowers drifting on a lazy breeze. The coolness of night was most welcome after their earlier terrifying experience in like to that of frazzled bacon on a griddle pan. She shuddered at the thought, but the memory of Ratchester attired in shirt and coat loaned to him by Edwin had lightened her mood.

As she ascended the staircase she recalled how they had all laughed despite the dire situation of the day's events, for Edwin at four inches taller than Rantchester, there was no denying a lot of shirt was tucked into the marquis' smutted breeches and the coat a little too long. Nonetheless with scrubbed face and his hair washed, to the casual eye he looked exquisitely dressed whilst seated in his carriage en route from Monkton to Hazel Grove. She too with face cleaned and gown shrouded beneath a makeshift lace tablecloth shawl, they had made it home without undue notice from passers-by.

She so regretted the loss of her pink gown for it was irretrievably ruined, and it was the very gown she had worn the day Edwin has first kissed her.

Upon entry to her bedchamber her personal maid appeared at her elbow and as much as she valued the other's unstinting loyalty, for the girl had left her family behind in London, she said, "I can manage tonight, Amy. Take an early night and read a book, I know you so love reading."

"Thank you, m' lady." Amy retreated as she always did, backwards, as though her mistress was of royal blood. Amy's slight frame and golden hair peeping beneath her mobcap was quite angelic, her blue eyes heaven sent. "Good night, m' lady."

The door closed and alone once again sense of loss overwhelmed her. How ridiculous to shed tears but she could not fight them back. If only, if only.

"Grandfather, grandfather," she said aloud, "will my life ever be free of death and destruction?"

But he was gone and would never be there to embrace her in times of need like this. Not as he had done so many times when life had taken wrong turns in her past.

Was she a harbinger of death?

She mopped the tears with a kerchief and sat on her bed, sense of dread washing over her. She sensed all was not well, sensed Edwin would not and could not come to her, and she dare not return to Abbeyfields for it would be madness without Rantchester at her side.

Her footmen were extremely street wise, London street-wise and both of goodly strength. She doubted not they would see right by her in anything asked of them. But she could not say or expect the same of her newly acquired coachman and two young grooms, for they were barely settled in their positions though certainly knowledgeable all things equine, livery and carriages.

What was she to do?

Laying her head to pillow she drew her legs up in a comforting and protective manner, her dark blue silk gown crushed in reckless manner. She closed her eyes, thoughts racing through events that had led to her ownership of Hazel Grove.

She would never forget the heartache endured as a child, the joys of being a young woman within elite circles, and then the despair of rejection by a society that once engaged her with heavy favour. But who could have foretold of a moonlit journey leading to the heady mix of falling in love with Edwin. And then to be brought full circle as though never absent from the *haut ton*, and all due to a brief encounter with Rantchester.

Morning already?

Awakening to birdsong was pure heaven; but fully clothed and a coverlet shrouding one's shameful laziness was utterly disgraceful.

She cast the coverlet aside and slipped from the bed and strolled to the left-window a smile flickering across her face. Amy had always had a good and caring heart, and had quite obviously slipped into the room and had not the courage to wake her mistress and chide her for crumpling her gown.

To see the sun rising to the east side of the house was impossible, but shadows of trees stretching horizontal across the meadows implied it was not long since dawn. She had not risen so early in a long while, and something from within compelled her to flee the house and run barefoot through dew-laden grass. She remembered a similar incident with her mother, and how her father had scolded both for such reckless and immodest behaviour. Oh how well she remembered that day of hitched up chemises, ankles bared and running like gypsy girls across a meadow at dawn.

She seated herself on a stool, stockings swiftly rolled from her legs. She then fled her room, fled down the staircase, unbolted the front door and ran across the grass to the meadow railings where her team of four had yet to rise from lazy equine abandonment. The grass beneath her feet was so wet and cool it was akin to treading on water. She turned, leaned her back against the iron railings and surveyed the lower part of her house.

It was modest as country houses go, of mellow sandstone and built some two hundred years previous, its layout representing the letter L, and she had loved it upon first sighting it.

Who couldn't fall in love with a house strewn with climbing roses, honeysuckle and flowering creepers?

With seven bedchambers not counting the servants' quarters it was possible to entertain in modest manner, and entertain she would. She glanced upward to her bedchamber windows and then from latticed window-to-window across the frontal façade. How strange. The shutters were closed in the far guest bedchamber.

She strolled back to the front door and upon entry she startled a maid scurrying past, both a little shaken in seeing each other so early of morn.

As she ascended the staircase her sighting of closed shutters lured her to the end bedchamber. About to open the door her heart leapt into her mouth for there was movement within, and if not mistaken it was the sound of a creaking bed frame. She held her breath, caught hold of the latch and very slowly lowered it until she was able to push the door slightly ajar.

A sigh of great relief escaped upon seeing Edwin in breeches and one stocking hose to foot. She stepped inside and asked in a whisper, "I had no notion you were here. What time did you arrive?"

"After midnight, and I thought for sure I would have to rouse a footman by making a terrible din, but Bannister had a bedroll in the hall and must have heard my horse. Did you know your stable-staff were standing watch as well?"

"Not at all, though Ratchester did have a word with the men about securing the house. I came up here and fell asleep whilst waiting for you."

"I know." He chuckled. "Hell of thing to ride through the dark and then find one's mistress asleep."

"If you came to my bedchamber, why did you leave?"

"It was for the best I slept in here. Believe me I would not have made for good company." He patted the bed gesturing for her to sit down. "Not long after you and Rantchester set off, Eliza's horse returned with a broken stirrup leather. I gathered as many men as able and set off to search for her in the direction the horse had galloped from. We found nothing and by late evening we turned back, and as we walked back up Monkton Hill the sky turned orange before us, yet the sun was setting at our backs. We knew before we reached the brow of the hill that the house was ablaze. Thankfully the household staff had escaped unharmed, but few possessions of worth from Abbeyfields could be saved. Hence there will be no trial, nor hangman's noose. The house is a burnt out ruin."

Felled by his statement she sat down beside him. "Eliza?"

"No hope of survival for the silly young thing. By the time we reached the house it was to see her standing at Adam's window. She looked down at us gathered below then closed the drapes."

"Oh Edwin, how dreadful, her dying that way?"

"Of course, but was it intentional or just acceptance of her fate?"

"She must have planned it. Why else would she ride away and then set her horse free if not to lure you from the house?"

He leaned forward elbows to knees; head in hands. "I've gone through it all so many times in my head I can no longer think straight."

She wrapped her arm about his waist and laid her head to his bare shoulder. "Where were you thinking of going, before I came in?"

"Back to Abbeyfields. There is much to be considered, and the Constable to be informed as to what occurred overnight. There is nothing to see, and no one to arrest."

"I can send word to the Constable, and you, my darling, need food and a few hours more of sleep before you can even propose a return to Abbeyfields."

He let fall his hands and laughed. "There is no Abbeyfields. The evil place is gone and I am free from its grasp." He leaned into her, kissed her hair. "I shall build a new house. What say you to a grand house on Monkton Hill?"

"Overlooking Abbeyfields?"

"I think not. We shall have it facing south to the river. I shall have trees planted to the east to shield the ruin from sight and let nature take its course in sealing the old place from view."

She eased her head from his shoulder, and not wanting to reveal inner disquiet at the prospect of a house on Monkton Hill, she asked, "And for now, shall you reside here, with me?"

"On one condition, as soon as banns can be read you become my wife."

"I think it only proper, for my reputation hereabouts, once talked of most hurtful, I am not sure I can weather harlot as my name again."

"Despite Adam's statement I have no mistress." He laughed, kissed her lips. "You had best away from my room right now, or Harlot may become you."

"Must I go?"

His answer was swift in action; pushed down to the bed, his second kiss was potent in deliverance. Harlot seemed most appropriate in the midst of rustling silk and eagerness of man to excite woman and vice versa.

The End.

~

153

Hazel Grove

Author Note:

~

Dear Reader,

I sincerely hope you enjoyed Georgette and Edwin's story. Part of the story is set within and around the City of Bath, but the delightful City of Wells (Somerset) had a vital role to play.

Famous street names will be familiar to ardent fans of Regency novels set within Bath, though I doubt few Regency novelists' have ventured to the ecclesiastical setting of Wells, which has a most beautiful cathedral and bishop's residence. The latter is surrounded by a moat, which is equally famous for its bell-ringing swans! As a child and adult I fed the swans of Wells (in my day), and derived much pleasure in walking the Cathedral Cloisters and that of the Chapter House Steps. So it is true to say, the city and surrounding area is very familiar to me.

~

Born in Somerset and having lived abroad in various places, there is a part of my heart that still abides in my home county. Perhaps that is why when characters appear within overnight dreams, and thus reveal their stories in cinematic glory, they have a secondary motive of bringing me home. Needless to say, the majority of my historical novels feature Somerset and many surrounding counties alongside London, and that of other foreign destinations that are often vital to respective plots.

If you enjoyed this novel you might also like Bath Series:

Book 2 in - The Dark Marquis,

starring Rupert Marquis of Rantchester as the hero.

Book 3 – Bath Series-
The Damnable Lady Caroline.
Again another murder mystery, this time the setting is a
castle in Scotland.

~
Single Novels & Novellas
To Risk All for Love
To Tempt a Duke
A Sinful Countess
Lady Louise de Winter
A Devilish Masquerade
The Duke's Gypsy
The Reluctant Duchess – Regency Murder Mystery
The Dissolute Rake (sequel)
The Earl's Captive Bride
Venetian Encounter – Georgian Murder Mystery
The Highwayman's Mistress
7 Shades of Sin (A Cardinal's Nightmare Begins)
Celeste – Gothic.
Highwayman Lord (sequel to Celeste)
Scandalous Whisper
Her Favoured Captain – (Warning Attempted Rape)
~
The Trevellians' of New-Lyn – Murder Mystery
Spanning two generations during the Georgian Period
&

17th century swashbuckling romances penned by Francine Howarth, are available at all Amazon web sites.

Debt of Honour (prequel novella)
By Loyalty Divided.
Toast of Clifton
Royal Secrets
Love & Rebellion
Lady of the Tower – Monmouth's Legacy
To come - Treason

Printed in Great Britain
by Amazon